MY SO-CALLED DEATH

One second, freshman Karen Vera's on top of the most fabulous cheer pyramid ever. The next, she's lying on the pavement with seriously unflattering cranial damage. Freakishly alive without a pulse, Karen learns that she's a genetically undead zombie.

Suddenly, Karen's non-life is an epic disaster. She's forced to attend a boarding school for the "death-challenged," her roommate is a hateful wannabe-goth weirdo, and she's chowing down on animal brains every day to prevent rot (um, ew?). Even worse, someone is attacking students and harvesting their brains for a forbidden dark ritual. And it might be the hottest guy at DEAD High, the one who makes Karen's non-beating heart flutter!

Armed with a perky smile and killer fashion sense, it's up to Karen to track down the brain snatcher and save her fellow students from certain zombie death.

Praise for Stacey Jay's
Megan Berry, Zombie Settler Series

"Sharp storytelling, good writing, and the current hunger for zombie fiction make this a sure hit with some nutritive value."
—*Booklist*

"…super entertaining.
Watch out for this fun new series!"
—*Romantic Times Magazine* (4 stars)

"…a cross between Stephenie Meyer and Joss Whedon…high-school angst with more than a dash of otherworldly danger."
—*Kidliterate Reviews*

"Part *Buffy the Vampire Slayer*, part *Night of the Living Dead*, this is one title you absolutely cannot miss."
—kidsblog.bookpeople.com

"…an impressive debut novel!"
—TheStorySiren.com

MY
SO-CALLED
DEATH

For Logan Anthony, my spider eater.

STACEY JAY

MY
SO-CALLED
DEATH

flux™

Woodbury, Minnesota

First Edition
First Printing, 2010

Book design by Steffani Sawyer
Cover design by Lisa Novak
Cover image © 2010 Rob Melnychuk/Digital Vision/PunchStock

Flux, an imprint of Llewellyn Publications

Library of Congress Cataloging-in-Publication Data
Jay, Stacey.
   My so-called death / Stacey Jay.—1st ed.
       p. cm.
   Summary: After dying in a cheerleading accident, high-school freshman Karen becomes a zombie and attends a boarding school for the undead, where she soon uncovers a murder mystery.
   ISBN 978-0-7387-1543-8
   [1. Zombies—Fiction. 2. Dead—Fiction. 3. Supernatural—Fiction. 4. Boarding schools—Fiction. 5. Schools—Fiction. 6. Mystery and detective stories.] I. Title.
   PZ7.J344My 2010
   [Fic]—dc22

                                        2009027696

Flux
Llewellyn Publications
A Division of Llewellyn Worldwide, Ltd.
2143 Wooddale Drive, Dept. 978-0-7387-1543-8
Woodbury, MN 55125-2989, U.S.A.
www.fluxnow.com

Printed in the United States of America

Acknowledgments

Thanks so much to Andrew Karre and Brian Farrey, my editors, and to all the people at Flux. You are amazing, professional, fun folks who have made this book a joy. Thanks to my agent, my sweet husband, preshush offspring, and amazing mom. And thanks to Liz Sutherland for being an exceptional lover of children, especially mine. You are a lifesaver, Liz! Thanks to my critique partners Stacia Kane and Julie Linker, Jill at Square Books Jr. for awesomeness, and all the booksellers who have been so wonderfully supportive in my first year as a published author. You all rock my casbah! Lastly, but not leastly, thanks to my readers. I love your emails and appreciate you all so very much. Thanks, thanks, and more thanks.

PROLOGUE

All in all, it was a good day to die. If there really is such a thing.

You hear characters in movies say that all the time, but does anyone *really* believe the words "good" and "die" belong in the same sentence?

Still, it could have been worse. It could have been a dark and spooky night instead of a beautiful Georgia evening in late October, with a light wind whipping across the Peachtree High football field, making zombies seem like the *last* thing anyone needed to worry about...

We were halfway through the second quarter and the Junior Varsity cheerleaders were kicking cheer tail with a pyramid of epic proportions. The entire squad was decked out in our new white and gold skirts and matching sweaters with gold pom-poms and shining gold scrunchies completing the look of absolute spirited gorgeosity.

There wasn't an eye in the stadium really paying attention to the lamo game as six sophomore girls based for three freshmen, who in turn hoisted another two freshmen on their shoulders. And then, like a rare and beautiful bird, the smallest of the freshman girls—a stunning five foot, one inch girl with golden-blond hair that does not often appear naturally in the twenty-first century and even more rarely on girls of half-Cuban ancestry—was basket tossed to the very top of the pyramid.

Her brown eyes flashed with triumph as she stuck the landing, her size 5½ sneakers sliding smoothly onto the waiting shoulders of the two freshman girls beneath her. Her muscled arms surged upwards into a V motion just as some player crossed the goal line, scoring six points for the Peachtree Peachpits Junior Varsity football team. The crowd went wild, and the girl knew it wasn't just because of the touchdown. They were in awe that a mere fourteen-year-old had nailed such a complex cheerleading maneuver.

I was that smallest freshman, with the blond hair, the brown eyes, and the "ego the size of Texas," according to my mother. She says I'm compensating for the fact that I was totally fugly until I grew into my nose. My dad thinks I have a Napoleon complex. I, however, prefer to think I have healthy self-esteem.

"Peachtree Peachpits! Go! Fight! Win!" I chanted along with the rest of the squad, our voices ringing with pride.

We were the only JV team in Georgia to *dare* such complicated stunts outside of cheer competitions with their abundance of professional spotters. As such, we never failed to intimidate the opposing cheer squad into the very dust. By halftime, those chicks were slinking from the field in disgrace.

The Peachtree JV cheerleaders were legendary, and I the most legendary of them all. There wasn't a freshman girl in school who didn't want to be me (at least for a day), and there wasn't a freshman guy who didn't knock himself out trying to look up my skirt when I landed at the top of the pyramid.

In fact, it was a boy trying to look up said skirt that *ruined* my life.

Just goes to show that Mom was right all along. Boys, as a species, are way overrated.

"Hey, Duke, Karen Vera's not wearing underpants. Look!" The shout was followed by a round of snorting from the benched portion of the Peachtree JV football team—which was a lot of boys, since the coach for JV was a softy who let any hopeless wannabe be on the team.

I scowled down my nose at the shouter, Kevin Jenkins, loser extraordinaire and total hanger-on to Duke Pearson, the studly sophomore I'd had my baby browns on ever since school started. No matter how irritated I was by this juvenile display, however, I did not for one *second* allow my tightly clenched muscles to loosen or my balance to falter. When one is at the top of a seventeen-foot pyramid, one cannot afford to let one's focus slip.

Unfortunately, I couldn't say the same for Rebecca and Madison, the two girls whose scrawny, unfocused shoulders I was standing upon. They looked up, for some reason feeling the need to check and see if I was indeed wearing my Spankies beneath my skirt—which I *was*, of course, duh—and that's when it all went to hell.

Hips tilted forward as heads tilted up, hips tilting led to feet tilting, feet tilting led to knees bending, which, in turn, led to the complete and absolute sabotage of the entire pyramid. As people in the stands screamed in horror, all seventeen feet of cheerleader wavered unsteadily, each girl shifting her weight to compensate for the girl above or beneath while the two frantic spotters behind us scrambled to put our wobbling mess of a stunt to rights.

Time slowed to a crawl as I pinwheeled my arms, desperately trying to triumph over gravity. But there was no way to stay on top. No matter how hard I tried, it was impossible to stand straight and tall on the shoulders of people who were suddenly *not there*.

I toppled backward, falling head first toward the black asphalt of the track. I didn't even have time to scream, just a split second to stare up into the sky, streaked with red from the setting sun, and wonder if Kevin Jenkins would feel properly guilt-ridden for killing me.

ONE

A genetic anomaly means that a gene has been modified by an accident called a mutation. This mutation changes the function of the gene, which gives information to the body that is different than the information received by the majority of human life forms.

Many Traditionally Alive people assume such a mutation can only lead to disease or death, but for the Death Challenged, our genetic anomaly leads to an entirely new way of life.

—*Total Health for the Death Challenged, 5th Edition*

———————

My very short-lived career at Peachtree High ended the day I fell from the top of the stunt pyramid and died. But didn't. That day I found out I wasn't ever going to die a normal death. Because I wasn't a normal person, I was a genetic anomaly. A mutation. A defect.

I'll stick with anomaly. It certainly sounds nicer, doesn't it? (Good thing I have that healthy self-esteem. Otherwise the whole "mutant" diagnosis could have done some major emotional damage.)

In brief, I am Death Challenged.

So what is Death Challenged, exactly?

Death Challenged is just a politically correct term—

like horizontally gifted (fat) or petroleum transfer technician (gas station attendant)—for a *zombie*. It didn't take me long to figure that one out, no matter how traumatized I was for the first twenty-four hours of my non-death.

There's just about nothing more terrifying than falling to your death and having your brains splattered all over the pavement. Unless it's falling to your *undeath* and having your brains splattered all over the pavement.

Thank god my parents were there in the stands supporting me, even though Dad is a professor of Medieval Literature who hates football and Mom spent most of the game on the grassy area near the stands letting the trips crawl around and drool on each other. (The trips are my one-year-old brothers and sister: Kyle, Keith, and Kimmy. My parents had triplets when I was thirteen. *And* they were goofy enough to name all of their children with K names. How lame are they? I'd be embarrassed to share if I weren't dedicated to historical accuracy, much like my professorial father.)

So Mom and Dad were there when the back of my skull burst open like a pomegranate seed and it looked like I'd bit the big one. But hadn't.

They both rushed to my side to find my brains all splattery and me without a pulse, but still mysteriously conscious and complaining that Kevin Jenkins deserved to have *his* head beaten to a bloody pulp for what he'd done. Luckily, my dad's research into our family's history had revealed some interesting phenomena when it came to our deaths—or nondeaths—so he wasn't too freaked.

Back in Cuba, Dad's great-great-aunt had been chased out of her seaside village for looking about twenty years old when she hit her sixtieth birthday. No matter how nice she was or how kick-ass her Ropa Vieja (literally "old clothes," but also a name for yummy shredded flank steak in a tomato-based sauce), the other villagers got creeped and thought she was a witch.

But according to family legend, this aunt survived the witch hunt and her flight from her native country and was still alive and kicking today, living somewhere in Venezuela. And she wasn't the only weirdo. There were others, including a great-great-great-grandfather in Spain and a ninety-year-old third cousin who could still pass for a man in his early thirties.

Dad had been trying to get in touch with all three for years to get the real story and separate fact from folklore, but had met with little success. Mom, of course, thought Dad was nuts and all the stories a bunch of bull-honkey. Until that day on the football field when her own daughter became one of the family freaks. Then she became a believer. Big time.

So while Mom hyperventilated and rounded up the trips and the crowd gasped and wept to see a beloved spirit leader so seriously injured, Dad scooped my brains back into my skull and hustled me to the car before the paramedics could arrive on the scene. Thank god he did. I mean, even the Death Challenged need brains to function. And I don't know what would have happened if normal people had figured out I was Undead.

I probably would have ended up in some sort of top-secret government experimental facility hooked up to a million tubes. The creepy men-in-black types would certainly have wanted to know why I was still chatting people up days after my heart stopped beating.

Instead, I got a visit from the principal of DEAD High herself, Theresa Samedi. The doorbell rang only seconds after we'd arrived home, and Dad opened the door to a very unique looking visitor.

"Don't worry. I know what's happened to your daughter, and I'm here to help."

Samedi's super-pale skin, short, spiky black hair, and long, flowing black dress would normally have freaked out my straight-laced dad big time. He's very anti-goth, and has been known to pass out fingernail-polish remover and notes suggesting counseling to college guys in his classes who do the black nail thing. My mom says he's just old-fashioned, but I think there might be a fingernail polish phobia involved. My grandmother has really long nails and is always touching up her manicure, even at the dinner table. Dad says the smell gives him a migraine, and he has to "take to his bed" for several days after Nana comes to visit. Issues, much? I say he should take a cue from himself and seek out the school counselor.

But I guess Samedi's words and the compassion in her big, almost black-brown eyes put Dad at ease, because he let her in, no questions asked. Luckily for curious individuals like myself, however, she explained her presence right away. Turns out she's super tuned in to the psychic vibrations of the Undead and knew the exact moment when I crossed the line from perky alive cheerleader to perky zombie splatter victim. (Just because you don't have a pulse doesn't mean you can't be perky.)

"You mean...she's dead, but she's not?" Dad asked, once introductions had been made and we were all comfy on the couches in our living room.

"No, she's dead," Principal Samedi said, ruffling her fingers through her spiked hair all casual-like. As if this weren't the worst news ever! "Her heart will never beat again, her core body temperature will be much lower than an average person's, and her skin will be vulnerable to rot if she doesn't take the proper precautions."

Ewww! Rot? For a second I thought I might yack at the very word, but then Samedi handed me a box of popcorn chicken—you've got to love it when company brings treats—and I realized I was famished. I mean, like, hungrier than I'd ever been in my life. I started scarfing while Principal Samedi chatted up my parents, explaining the genetic mutation stuff.

"When we become something society cannot accept, we must find a new society." Samedi smiled and handed my parents some pretty colored brochures showing all these happy zombie kids studying up on a new way of death at DEAD High. That really *is* the name of the school. The institute of Death Challenged Education for Adolescents and the Deprogrammed.

"A school? For...dead people?" Mom asked, looking understandably freaked.

"Undead adolescents," Samedi corrected. "There are schools for educating those who become Undead later in life, but DEAD High is strictly for teenagers in seventh through twelfth grades. We're the oldest Undead boarding school in the central United States."

"We've never considered boarding school. We want Karen at home," Mom said, struggling to concentrate while the trips crawled all over her, whining and fussing.

My sister and brothers sensed something was wrong, and, in their babyness, had decided being held by Mom was the only thing that would give them comfort. Too bad she didn't have a few extra arms. Humans were clearly not designed for the "more than one baby at a time" thing. I didn't know what god was smoking when he decided my mom needed *three* little blessings at the ripe old age of thirty-seven.

"I'm afraid it will no longer be possible for Karen to live with you, or in the human world at all," Samedi said in her calm, authoritative voice.

"Excuse me, but who are you to tell me what is or isn't possible for my daughter?" Mom asked in her less calm but equally authoritative voice.

"Let's hear Principal Samedi out. We're out of our element here, honey." Dad plucked Kimmy from Mom's lap, begging her with his eyes not to pick a fight with the creepy zombie lady. In that second, I saw that he was scared of Samedi. This probably would have made me scared of her too (my dad's no wimp, despite his glasses and aversion to strenuous exercise) if the popcorn chicken I was chowing wasn't so amazingly yummy. I mean, how could a woman who brought such hot, greasy goodness be bad?

"Yes, please. Do let me explain." Samedi leaned closer to Mom and Mom chilled out, almost like Samedi had hypnotized her or something. I'd certainly never seen my mom recover from pissed-offedness so quickly before. But maybe she was just going into a mild state of shock. Death—even when it was an "undeath"—probably had that effect on a lot of people. "Over the centuries, the Death Challenged have learned that we must keep a low profile. Integration with living society is simply not possible for our kind. It isn't safe for us to reveal our true nature."

"Because people are afraid. Intolerant of anything extremely different," Dad said, in his professor voice.

"Exactly. Invariably, the Undead are hunted out and destroyed, no matter how civilized our behavior or how earnestly we seek to integrate ourselves into the human world." Samedi's words sent a little chill down my spine as visions of zombie-hating mobs danced through my head.

Mobs. Not a good thing. Unless it's a mob gathered at a pep rally to get psyched up for a big game, and even then you have to be careful. School spirit can be as destructive as any other deep, passionate emotion if it's allowed to get out of hand.

"So we've created several secret schools, places where young people can complete their conventional education while also learning the skills they'll need to survive and thrive as a member of the Death Challenged community. Our world is...different, and Karen will need help to adjust."

"So how much does this school cost?" Dad, ever the practical member of our family. "Karen has a small college fund, but we'd planned on her getting free tuition at the university where I teach, so—"

"The school is fully funded by donations from older, established members of our community. There will be no out-of-pocket expenses for your family, aside from school supplies and whatever Karen will need to make her dorm room comfortable."

Dorm room? Ugh, did I want to live in a dorm room?

I wasn't sure, but I seemed unable to concentrate on anything but shoveling more chicken in my mouth. Dang, but the stuff was good. Addictive, even. I could see it replacing chocolate as my number one food jones.

"I promise you, Mr. Vera," Samedi said, laying a small, white hand on Dad's arm, "Karen will be well taken care of."

"What if we say no? What if we think Karen should stay with us?" Mom asked, seeming to come out of her trance when Samedi shifted her attention to my dad.

My new principal turned her slightly less friendly black-brown eyes back to Mom. I swear I could feel the room get a little colder. Samedi was nice, but man, I wouldn't want to be on her bad side. "Once the funeral has been held and—"

"Funeral?" Mom's volume made the trips start fussing even more, but I could still hear Samedi's calm voice over the din.

"Karen will have to have a funeral and be mourned by her loved ones as if she has passed on. She must be dead in the living world's eyes."

"But I—"

"She will be able to return home to visit," Samedi said, calming my mom down a bit. "That is, assuming your family observes the rules of our community and Karen learns to cloak her true appearance with the proper illusion spell."

"We can do magic? Like witches?" I asked.

"No, nothing like witches."

Well. Kill that buzz before it even got started.

"Our magic is based in death, in darkness, and as a consequence is unpredictable and dangerous." Samedi's voice held a warning I didn't understand. "You will be instructed in basic spells that will facilitate your continued interaction with your family and the human world. Nothing more."

"So she gets to be human and come home. Why are we faking a funeral?" Mom asked, her frustration clear.

Samedi sighed. "Karen will be able to interact with the human world, but she will never *be* human and she will never be known to humans as Karen Vera. The High Council of the United States will not allow it. She will have to assume another identity."

"So you're telling me I've lost my daughter."

"Mom, you haven't lost me," I said, snapped out of my chicken-chomping haze by the sound of tears in Mom's voice. "I'm right here. It's just a new school."

"Right. Just a new school." My mom started crying for real, but then the triplets started screaming and wailing and tearing each other's hair out in a prelude to their own feeding frenzy (hungry babies, nearly as scary as hungry zombies), and she had to pull it together.

Surprisingly, she seemed mostly okay by the time she fetched the trips some Cheerios to gnaw on while she cooked macaroni and cheese. Mourning my loss came second to feeding my siblings—which hurt, despite the fact that I was glad to see Mom chill out.

"I know this is a lot to take in," Samedi said in a hushed voice, like she didn't want Mom, who was busy in the kitchen, to hear what she was saying. "But we are the only facility in our area equipped to provide for Karen's continuing education while preparing her for the unique needs of her Death Challenged life."

"What kind of unique needs?" I asked around a mouthful of food, assuming it was okay to talk with my mouth full since I'd just been through a traumatic event.

"Well, for one thing, your physical body is now even more precious than it was before," Samedi said, addressing me in the same tone she'd used with Dad, winning her big points in my book. "You could potentially live for hundreds of years, and you're going to have to learn to take very good care of your mortal flesh."

Hmmm ... hundreds of years. That could be cool.

"You'll also run the risk of being confused with black magically raised zombies." She then went on to explain how black magically raised zombies are mindless, scary, red-glowing-eyed freaks who want to chow on human flesh and not much else.

"And I thought they were only in Romero films," Dad said, earning a chuckle from the principal.

Some old person joke, I guessed, continuing to munch.

"No, they're real. And there are paranormally gifted humans who devote their lives to slaying the creatures." Samedi's smile faded as she continued. "Some of them know about the Death Challenged and will take the time to differentiate between the two. But there are others who believe any Undead who refuses to return to the grave deserves to be destroyed."

"Destroyed like ... killed for real?" A shiver ran down my spine when she nodded. So my zombie mob fears were not unfounded.

"I'm afraid so. And I've only attracted more negative attention with my work with the Deprogrammed teens in the area," she said.

"They're different than the Death Challenged kids?" I asked.

Samedi nodded. "Sometimes, black magically raised zombies can have their soul returned to their body if their corpse was raised within a year of their death. And if the proper spells are employed before they develop a taste for human blood."

Ugh. Taste for human blood. Gross. Finally, my chicken craving began to fade.

"Those who hunt the Undead consider the Deprogrammed abominations who will eventually return to the murderous business they were raised for, but I haven't found that to be the case. Once the dark power that controls the black magically raised is banished, many go on to lead existences very similar to the naturally Death Challenged. A number of them even study at our school."

Things got quiet for a moment as Samedi let all that info sink in, Dad adjusted his glasses ten more times, and I returned to shoveling in the popcorn chicken until my cardboard box was empty. Finally Dad broke the silence.

"I've done some research about extended life in my family, but I have no idea how to help Karen through this." He looked stressed out and excited at the same time. "I think attending your school would be for the best. What do you think, honey?"

What did I think? I still had a hole in the back of my head where my brains would spill out if I bent over too far. Was I even capable of thinking, let alone making good decisions?

Although, if I'd understood Samedi correctly, there wasn't really a decision to be made. I either faked my death and transferred to her school or … disappeared? She'd said I wouldn't be allowed to live as Karen Vera anymore because of some big, United States-wide rule.

Personally, I didn't want to find out what would happen to me if I refused to follow that rule. I had a feeling the consequences wouldn't be pleasant. Besides, I was a rule follower from way back. Even in preschool I'd gotten gold stars for sharing my paste and being the first to lie down and snooze when the teacher hit the lights for naptime.

"Well … I can't go back to PHS if I'm dead. So I guess you'd better sign me up."

"A wise choice." Principal Samedi smiled and then dove right into what would need to be done to get me enrolled in the high school for the zombified.

First of all, I was going to have to be officially declared dead to everyone I'd known before, except for my immediate family. There would have to be a funeral and mourning and an obituary and everything. My dad was a little concerned about how he was going to fake my death without a body, but Principal Samedi said she would take care of all that with her connection down at the coroner's office. Right after she introduced me to my new roomie at DEAD.

"Then I'll have my assistant issue Karen's uniforms and get to work on her class schedule." Samedi smiled and rose from the couch, signaling that our business here was done. "That way, Karen won't have to miss any school as a result of her unfortunate accident."

Okay, so, let's recap:

1. Dead to everyone I used to know, including my best friend, Piper.
2. No longer allowed to go to real school or cheer on my cheer squad.

3. Must now attend strange school where I know no one.
4. Must now wear *uniforms* at strange school where I know no one.
5. Must room with stranger at this strange school where I know no one.
6. Will not even get to miss a single freaking day of classes as a result of falling off a cheer pyramid and having my skull cracked open like an egg on drugs. (Or whatever that old commercial was … the one on VH1's 1980s special.)

And as if that weren't bad enough, Principal Samedi took that moment to drop the food bomb. I was reaching for a bowl of mac and cheese from the tray Mom brought into the living room when I was told I would no longer be allowed to eat real food. *Any* real food, with the exception of various forms of raw meat. Turns out that dairy, sugar, fruits, vegetables, and just about anything else yummy wreaks havoc on the Undead's digestion.

"But what about the popcorn chicken? It wasn't raw," I said, determined to find a loophole in the no-food rule. I mean, I *love* food. And chocolate! Geez. How was I expected to live—or at least not die—without chocolate?!

That's when Principal Samedi told me about brains. That eating brains was necessary to keep my body in good working order and prevent rot, and that I would be eating them for the rest of my death.

Not only that, but I had already *been* eating them for the past fifteen minutes.

I ran to the bathroom and tried to throw up, but it turned out that my newly Undead body had already metabolized the brains.

Ewwwww...brains.

I looked at myself in the mirror and did my best imitation of a horror movie creature, groaning "braiiinnnnsssss" to my pale reflection. Then I sat on the toilet and cried until Principal Samedi knocked on the door and told me it was time for us to go.

Turns out tears are not exclusively for the living. Yippee.

TWO

Respecting your new roommate is essential. Now that you are one of the Undead, you could conceivably live for hundreds of years. The relationships you begin now will be the friendships that carry you through the millennium. Remember that, and conduct yourselves accordingly.

—*Dorm Handbook for Incoming Students,*
DEAD High

Wanted: White noise machine, will pay any price. Would be awesome if it had one of those aromatherapy things too. My roommate snores and smells! Pleaz help! Am exhausted and nasally tormented!

—*Note on girls' dorm bulletin board*

Clarice sucks butt.

—*Bathroom stall, second floor girls' bathroom*

———————

"What are you doing? Is that a *cheerleader* on my wall?" The shriek from the doorway made me scream and then burst out laughing.

I always laugh when I'm scared. I probably would have laughed as I was falling off the cheer pyramid if there had been time. Admittedly weird, but my friends back in my human life thought it was funny that I giggled all the way through horror movies.

"What are you laughing at? That has to come down." The girl in the door glared at the United Cheerleader Association calendar I'd hung on my side of the room. She threw her sweater on the floor. Her greasy, shoulder-length black hair twitched angrily around her shoulders and her heavily lined gray eyes narrowed like I was a maggot she'd just spotted on her arm.

Maggots are a zombie's only natural predator—aside from angry mobs of humans or the supernatural-slayer types. Principal Samedi had already warned me to watch out for flies that love to lay their eggs in Undead flesh because, once they get started, maggot infestations can be almost impossible to get under control.

Ugh. *Maggot infestation.* If there was a grosser combination of words in the English language I couldn't think of it.

The thought made me laugh again. I was in a laugh-or-cry situation. I had to keep giggling or I was going to lose what was left of my sense of humor.

"Ohmygod, what is *wrong* with you?" the girl asked, wrinkling her upper lip.

Guess she didn't share my human friends' appreciation for ill-timed chortling.

No wonder, really. This chick didn't look like she smiled. Ever. She'd already acquired a frown line between her eyebrows—though she couldn't have been more than fifteen—and her lips turned down in a scowl that she'd clearly worked hours on perfecting. It's not easy to get the sides of your mouth to turn down like that. Unless you're a toddler on the verge of a temper tantrum.

The girl stomped her foot, doing an excellent impression of a two-year-old. "Hello? Can you talk? I asked you what the hell you were doing here."

"That's the first time you've said hello." I propped my hands on my hips, determined not to take any psycho from this freak.

I'd already died, become Undead, eaten brains, been forced to leave the bosom of my family, and endured the stares of the entire second floor of the girls' dorm as I carried my things down the hall. I was done with bad stuff. From here on out, this night was going to get better. It had to, or I was going to lose it and call my mom and beg her to come pick me up and take me home no matter what the High Council of brain munchers had to say about it.

"Get out. Take your cheerleader crap and that pink … *thing* and Get. Out." She pointed one jabby little finger toward the door and her scowl deepened. "I don't room with anyone, let alone some blond bimbo cheer freak with pink bedding."

Ah. So this was Clarice.

Clarice, who Principal Samedi had assured me was going to be thrilled to finally have a roommate. Clarice, who was also a freshman and would love to help me get caught up on the work I'd missed so far this semester. Clarice, who the bathroom stall had warned me "sucked butt."

Of the three things I'd heard, the last one was the only one I was willing to believe.

"This is where I was told to put my things," I said, my stomach cramping as I realized I was going to have to *live* with this nasty little troll. What had I done to deserve this? Been born blond and cute, with a love for the color pink? I couldn't help any of those things. Even loving pink was genetic. It was only a matter of time until that was proven by science. "I'm sorry if you don't like pink, but—"

"It makes me want to vomit. And your sweater looks like a unicorn puked all over it."

"This is the only bedspread that I brought with me." I returned her glare, deciding it was best to ignore her commentary on my outfit. There was no point discussing fashion with a girl with enough grease in her hair to fuel the deep frier down at McDonald's. Besides, my sweater was cute. Purple was totally the new black, and the glitter was intentionally ironic. "I can look for something else next time I go home, but—"

"Oh, you're going, all right. Right now. I'm calling the RA."

"Go ahead and call the RA." RA? What was the RA? Rabid Animal? Random Android? Rebel Anteater? "But Principal Samedi said this was the only space free on the second floor."

"Then they can put you on the third floor with the juniors and seniors," Clarice said, before raising her voice to a scream.

I winced and covered my ears. I couldn't tell exactly what she was yelling, but it sounded like she was calling for a "manatee," confirming my suspicion that she was completely out of her mind. Manatees do not live on land, even at zombie schools. I might be new, but I wasn't born yesterday.

I was getting ready to tell Clarice that her cries for a sea cow to come to her rescue were in vain when a pretty girl with bright red hair and a smattering of brown freckles across her pale, Undead nose appeared in the doorway.

Most people wouldn't have realized she was Death Challenged, but I was starting to be able to tell who was and who wasn't a zombie within a few seconds of meeting them. It was almost like I'd acquired a sixth sense where the Undead were concerned. I just *knew* who was my kind and who wasn't. Kind of like I'd just *known* when a girl from another school was a cheerleader, even if she wasn't in uniform. There's just something in the perky tilt of the chin that gives away the inner school spirit.

"Hey, Clarice! So this is your new roommate." The new girl smiled widely, as if she didn't notice Clarice's scowl, and held out her hand. "I'm Mandy Dee, one of the Resident Assistants for the second floor, seventh grade through sophomore year."

Oh. Mandy Dee, not manatee, and an RA was a Resident Assistant, not a Rabid Animal. Still, I wasn't giving Clarice any *Get Out of Crazyville Free* cards. So far she'd been the rudest person I'd ever met, which meant she was either crazy or an epic jerk. Out of the kindness of my heart, I was willing to call her crazy. A person can't help being crazy. Epic jerkiness, however, is another matter entirely.

"Karen Vera," I said, taking the offered hand and shaking it, though it felt decidedly weird. Had I ever shaken someone's hand? I couldn't remember. I couldn't seem to remember anything now. Maybe my brains *had* been irreparably damaged in the accident.

"What a pretty name, and I love your sweater. You're going to fit right in," Mandy Dee said with another smile. "So how are you?"

"I'm good, really good." I'd just *died* and found out I had the roommate from hell; how good could I be? I wasn't good, but I couldn't tell Mandy Dee that, not when I could tell she loved it here at zombie school.

"Settling in okay?"

"Well, I—"

"No, she's not. She's not going to settle in at all. I told Principal Samedi I can't have a roommate, especially *her*," Clarice said, inserting her angry little body between me and Mandy Dee. "It's just not possible. She's got to go."

"This is the only bed free, Clarice," Mandy Dee said in a logical, perky voice. "There's nowhere else for Karen to go." Her eyes slid to mine for a second and I read the pity there, confirming my suspicion that Clarice didn't get any more likable after prolonged exposure.

"She can go up a floor, can't she?" Clarice's whine made me wince. "There are rooms free up there. Entire *rooms*."

"Those are only for upperclassmen."

"But—"

"Clarice, please."

"But she's a *cheerleader*! Look at that stupid thing on the wall!"

"There's really nothing I can do," Mandy said, looking straight at me, though Clarice was the one protesting our roommate status. "They're working on getting some extra space approved for students on the first floor, but right now those rooms are only for female faculty."

"This sucks!" Clarice made a sound somewhere between a scream and a growl and hurled herself onto the bed on the other side of the room. The bed that was covered with a black bedspread, black pillows, and a black afghan draped across the end.

Geez. I should have known me and the roomie weren't going to get along. My sweater might look like a unicorn puked on it, but Clarice's bed looked like the inside of an emo vampire's lair. And emo vampires and unicorns do *not* get along. One is a creature of light and the other a minion of angst-ridden darkness. (But a unicorn would totally win in a fight. One big, sharp horn trumps two tiny fangs any day.)

"Listen, Clarice," I said, willing to give reason one last chance. I had to live with this girl, after all, and it would be a heck of a lot easier if she would stop acting like my cheer calendar and I were harbingers of the plague. "I've never had to share a room before, either, but I'm sure we can make this—"

"Shut up, you freak!" Clarice snatched the afghan from the edge of her bed and pulled it over her head.

Oh my god. She was hiding under her *blankie*. It was so ridiculous I would have laughed if the lump under the afghan hadn't started shaking. Sobbing sounds trickled out from underneath. The girl was crying, *crying* because she was going to be forced to room with me.

I can safely say I'd never felt so repulsive. Even knowing the girl losing it across the room was a nutcase didn't help. I hadn't expected to be immediate BFFs with my room-mate, but I hadn't expected this either. This was ... horrible! Clarice and her freaky black bed and nasty grease head and chipped black fingernails had finally finished the job of making this the worst day of my entire life. Bar none.

"Oh gosh, Karen. Don't cry. I promise you, this will get better," Mandy Dee said with a tentative pat on my arm. "Clarice gets upset easily, but she—"

"Don't talk about me like I'm not here!" Clarice yelled from under her blanket, her words ending in a strangled sob.

"Really, it won't be that bad," our RA continued in a whisper. "She's all bark and—"

"I am not! I am not all bark. I bite, and I'll bite *her* if you let her stay here!" After those encouraging words, Clarice fell completely apart, sobbing so hysterically you would have thought the powers that be were forcing her to room with a freak with infectious boils, not a perfectly clean natural blond.

For some reason, hearing her crying harder made me start crying harder too, and pretty soon I couldn't even hear what Mandy Dee was saying as she flipped off the lights and backed out of the room. All I could hear was the sound of my own nonbeating heart breaking as I hurled myself onto my pink bed and sobbed until the exhaustion of the day finally got to me.

As my eyes slid closed, I worried for a second that Clarice would try to kill me in my sleep, but then I remembered I was already dead—or Undead—and it probably wouldn't matter if she did. I was mostly indestructible and likely to be around for a very long time.

Which didn't sound so great right now. Life had just been getting weirder and weirder from the second I'd died. I had a feeling the only thing I could count on was that the weirdness would continue.

And I didn't like weirdness. Not one little bit.

THREE

In our darkest hours,
when the sound of a nonbeating heart is as loud
in its absence as the hooves of many thousand
    Roman horses,
still we remain, the Undead, the Undeniable,
sons and daughters of the first Egypt.

—*Akori, ancient Egyptian slave & third generation
Undead, Zombie Poets Through the Ages, 2nd edition*

"You're going to have to take that off before lunch," Trish warned as she threw the books from her morning classes in her locker and brushed her straight brown bangs out of her face. The look in her eyes was completely serious, but I still couldn't keep from smiling.

I had a new friend! Before the events of last night, that wouldn't have been such a big deal. I made friends easily and often. But after eight fitful hours breathing the same air as Clarice the Psychotic and Evil, listening to her sob and mutter to herself under her blanket all night, I had a new appreciation for friendly faces.

Trish was well on her way to being my new BFF. So far, I loved the girl like a zombie loves brains. She was excessively funny and friendly and had gone out of her way to make my first morning at DEAD an absolute breeze. Not only did I get a guided tour of the campus after breakfast—complete with advice on the best places to scope drool-worthy Undead guys—but she had saved me from severe embarrassment during first period when Mr. Cork initiated some unsolicited teacher-student bonding.

Mr. Cork, the English and Zombie Poets teacher, was nearly six feet tall but probably didn't weigh much more than I did. He was so skinny he practically disappeared when he turned sideways, and looked like a skeleton who had shoplifted a set of bulgy eyes from a dead fish. And he smelled nearly as bad. The man *reeked* of cologne, like he'd taken a bath in *Stinky Cowboy Dipped in Melted Cinnamon Number 5* or something equally heinous. It was seriously all I could do not to throw up my brain cakes when he'd put his arm around me, pinning me to his side while he tried to figure out who he should move so that I could have one of the chairs near the front, the better to help me catch up on all the zombie poetry I'd missed in the first nine weeks of school.

Thankfully, Trish had raised her hand almost immediately, offering her chair and moving to the back, proving she hadn't just hung around with me so far because it had been her turn to play tour guide. She actually liked me and, like a true friend, wanted to spare me the torture of standing within two feet of Mr. Cork any longer than necessary.

We were *obviously* kindred spirits, even though I was naturally Death Challenged and Trish was Deprogrammed.

But was I ever glad she was. It was just too awful to think of her dying at fourteen because her friend's mom's car was hit by a drunk driver. (People who drink and drive are total wastes, and I would gladly eat their brains. Zombies are supposed to stick to animal brains, but I think they should make an exception for certain wastes of human flesh like drunk drivers and murderers and people who lie about getting to second base.)

Of course, since no one in Trish's family had any clue zombies were real, her mom was way more freaked than my parents when the people from DEAD showed up on her front doorstep one dark and rainy night with the daughter she'd buried a couple of months before. Her mom had started screaming and eventually had to be sedated. It had taken three days for Principal Samedi to convince Trish's mom that Trish's body had been raised by a voodoo priest and then Deprogrammed by Principal Samedi. It took another four days to convince her to send Trish to zombie school.

I was a little jealous, honestly. My parents had been way too cool about the whole zombie business, making me wonder if they'd been looking for an excuse to ship me off to boarding school even before my accident.

The thought made my smile fade.

"I'm serious, K. You're going to get in trouble." Trish's dark brown eyes landed pointedly on my chest and then turned to check her chin-length bob in her locker mirror. "Principal Samedi is on lunch duty today and she gets seriously distressed about uniform violations."

"This isn't a uniform, it's a fashion emergency," I protested, nevertheless removing my very gangsta-esque silver skull-and-crossbones necklace and shoving it in my locker before trailing Trish down the hall toward the cafeteria.

I'd worn the thing more as an act of protest than a fashion statement, anyway. It was a remnant from a long-ago Halloween and the only thing I could find in my jewelry box that was big enough not to get lost amidst the yards of black fabric that swirled around my body and all the way to the floor.

The black choir robe-ish uniform was crushing my will to live, and it was only my first day of classes. Unlike Trish, who was five feet ten inches tall and had the kind of clothes-hanger-like model's body that could make even the DEAD high uniform look decent, I looked like a black blob. An incredibly pale and short black blob, since even the smallest-size robe was still a little too big, and my Undead skin looked even more Undead when contrasted with something so dark.

Of course, I knew it could be worse. I could be a male of the species forced to wear the atrocity.

DEAD issued the same uniform for both sexes, in some sort of equality thing that was just too cruel and unusually evil for words. The boys looked like sinister Friar Tucks. Or members of the same depressing choir as the girls. But at least the girls were allowed to wear conservative makeup and hair accessories; the boys just looked … sad.

I'd clipped an obnoxiously pink bow in my hair this

morning just to make a statement—and to annoy Clarice, of course. *If you can't be good friends, be good at being enemies* was my new motto, and I planned to make my roomie's nights as miserable as she made mine.

Luckily, me making Clarice miserable had also made Trish laugh. She'd loved the bow-paired-with-sparkly-crossbones look and insisted we do lunch together.

I was grateful for the invite since kindred spirits seemed in short supply at DEAD. Over half the school had the creepy goth thing going on big time. Which, I'm sorry, but, cliché much? We were zombies. I was being way more rebellious and societal-norm-rejecting by wearing a pink bow than the goth minions were with their black eyeliner and purple fingernails.

Trish was on the same page—she wore only the slightest smudge of brown eyeliner on her top lids and very fashion-forward lip-gloss. Still, she attracted her share of attention, since she was by far the tallest girl in the school. I, of course, was one of the shortest—even shorter than most of the seventh and eighth graders—so we were a bit of an odd-looking pair.

The height difference wouldn't have bothered me *that* much in my old life, but now that I knew I would never get any taller, it sort of made me sad to have to look up to nearly everyone else in the world. I'd always assumed I would get a growth spurt and end up at least five five. Now I'd always be a rather runty five one.

But on the bright side, at least I'd died at fourteen and

not any younger. Due to the aging process of zombified skin—which just isn't as fresh and nubile looking as the real thing, no matter how many brains you eat—I would be able to pass as an adult in the human world in a few years, as long as I used an illusion spell to make sure I wasn't recognized by anyone from my old life. I'd be able to get a driver's license and vote and maybe even get married ... if I met an Undead guy worth looking at twice, let alone hooking up with for eternity.

So far, the Death Challenged dudes were not so dreamy.

Except for *him*, of course.

"Ladies, might I interest you in a menu?" The sex god himself sat on a stool just inside the door to the cafeteria, handing out little paper menus and punching lunch cards. Not even the dorky cafeteria-worker hat he wore was able to detract from his complete hotness.

Gavin McDougal. Sigh ... more like Gavin McDoMe.

He was by far the best-looking guy I'd ever seen in real life—Death Challenged or average human. His black hair was just long enough to hang in his bright blue eyes, and his almost-too-perfect face was softened by the cutest set of dimples in the world. Even deathly pale skin couldn't make Gavin anything but entirely yummy. He also happened to be one of the smartest guys in the junior class and had lettered in swimming two years running.

Swim team was one of the only sports offered at DEAD—aside from distance running, a leftover from a time when zombies spent most of their time running away from angry human mobs. Other sports were considered too unsafe for the Undead. We can heal most injuries if we get the proper amount of brainy nutrition, but head trauma can occasionally do permanent and gruesome damage. Considering we have to make do with the bodies we have for the rest of our very long lives, it makes sense to be careful with the earthly shell. So swimming and running were the only organized athletic options. No contact sports, no high-risk athletics, and certainly no cheerleading. Sob!

But really, what would be the point? It's not like the runners would be around long enough to hear the cheers, and swimmers couldn't admire perky stunts with their heads underwater. And, I came to find out, my accident wasn't the first case of zombification by cheering. Cheer zombies were more common than shark-attack-induced Undead and lightning-strike-induced Undead combined.

Which was good to know…though there was still no way I was getting in the ocean. I'd watched *When Animals Attack* on the Discovery Channel and was properly afraid of things (like sharks) that had teeth as big as my hand.

"No, I don't need a menu," Trish said, grinning at Gavin. She thought he was the hottest thing going at DEAD, too. We'd discussed his fabulousness in depth over breakfast. "I'm going raw line. I cut myself shaving last night and need a quick fix."

Zombie hair and fingernails grow after death, which is pretty cool. I'd hate to think I'd be doomed to a lifetime of skanky nails if I broke one off opening my locker.

"And what about you, Karen? Menu?" McDoMe asked as he punched Trish's lunch card. He knew my name! And we hadn't even been introduced! He must have asked someone about me, or at the very least paid attention to the "new girl" gossip.

"Yeah, I'll take one," I said, trying not to let my grin get too goofy when Gavin's fingers brushed mine as he handed over the slip of paper.

Menu Tuesday Lunch

The raw line:
Cow brains and ground beef with a side of shaved tuna.

The hot line:
Popcorn pig brain bites with a side of
raw seasoned sausage served in intestines.

"I did the raw thing this morning," I said, batting my eyes. "So I guess I can check out the hot line. Right?"

I already knew that the raw line was only mandatory if you had a cut or bruise or your skin had started to rot—because raw brains and meat helped the Death Challenged heal more quickly than cooked—but I wasn't about to pass up a chance to get some older and wiser advice from my new crush.

"Yeah, you should be fine to go hot." He punched my lunch card, grinning in a way that made my addled brain certain there was more to those words than met the ear.

Maybe he'd meant I should be fine to go with the hot

line because *I* was so hot. Because I was irresistible to his older, cooler self despite the fact that I was a newbie, a freshman, and looked like a little black rain cloud in my heinous school uniform.

Now, any second he was going to hand back my lunch card and our fingers would brush again. But this time, he wouldn't let go! This time, he would keep holding my hand, abandoning his post so that he could personally escort me to fetch my plate of pig brain bites and—

"Oh my god! Kendra's dead!!" The lunch lady's scream was met by a round of giggles at first because … um, hello? We are *all* dead or we wouldn't be attending DEAD High or trolling for brains in the DEAD lunchroom.

But then she screamed again, and again, and just kept on screaming until finally Principal Samedi—who had been disciplining someone who had dared dye their hair a non-regulatory orange—raced across the lunchroom. The kids waiting in line for the raw meal moved to make way for the stiff-featured principal and her stiffer spiked hair as she strode behind the lunch counter and disappeared into the kitchen.

Seconds passed in silence, the entire lunchroom as eerily quiet as the tombs we would have all been lying in if we weren't Undead. Then, Principal Samedi, her face whiter than the white high priestess' robe she wore when she was officially on duty, appeared in the doorway.

She took a deep breath and brought a shaking hand to her lips. She looked like she was about to lose her lunch.

Considering zombies metabolize at an alarmingly fast rate, that was probably impossible, but it didn't make the gesture any less disturbing.

Unfortunately, the words out of our fearless leader's lips were even *more* disturbing.

"I have never lied to my students and I don't intend to start now, but I will warn you that what I'm about to say is frightening in the extreme. That said, I don't want anyone to lose their composure. Whoever did this will be dealt with. I promise you that." Another deep breath, and the principal's eyes closed, as if she couldn't stand to look us in the eye while she spilled the big, scary beans. "Kendra Duncan has had her cranium fully harvested. If we don't find her brain within the next few days, she won't be... won't be returning to us."

For a moment I thought maybe Samedi just meant that Kendra (a sophomore who worked the raw line, I'd met her that morning) wouldn't be returning to DEAD High. Then my slow-on-the-uptake brain remembered what "cranium harvesting" meant.

It meant her brain had been removed. I'd learned all about the cranium harvesting of pigs and cows in health class just two periods ago. But this wasn't a pig or a cow. This was Kendra, a girl I'd seen headed down to the girls' showers this morning, a girl who'd actually remembered my name and said "Hi" to the new freshman in the hall. And someone had *harvested* her brain.

"Everyone return to your dorms immediately," Principal Samedi announced. "Afternoon classes are cancelled. Do not leave your rooms if it can be avoided. And if you must leave your room, do not, I repeat *do not* venture out alone. The person responsible for this could still be on campus."

If I'd eaten anything since breakfast, I know I would have defied the rules of nature and zombie metabolism and spewed all over McDoMe's shoes. As it was, I just leaned over and hyperventilated for a few minutes, giving me plenty of time to observe that Gavin's shoes were not regulation uniform gear. We all had to wear brown or black loafers or boots, but he was wearing Converse one stars—and those non-regulation shoes were splattered with blood.

FOUR

The average Undead male requires X milligrams of brains daily.

The average Undead female requires Y milligrams of brains daily.

If X is a prime number less than ten and Y is equal to X-1, what is the value of X?

—Undead and Uneasy with Numbers:
A User-friendly Algebra Review

———————

"I'm fine, Mom. I swear," I said, rolling my eyes at Trish, who sat at the end of my bed painting her toenails a shade of pink as bright and cheery as my quilt. Her math homework lay on the floor next to mine, both of them unfinished. Who could concentrate on remedial algebra after the day we'd had? "I just wanted to call so you wouldn't worry when Principal Samedi calls the house tonight. She says she's going to let all the parents know what happened."

"She'd better let all the parents know. Some girl was killed at—" A wail sounded from the background and Mom sighed in obvious frustration. "Kimmy! Stop that, don't bite your brother."

"Well, she wasn't really killed," I said. "She'll be fine if they find her brain and put it back in within the next few days." Though what were the chances of that happening? Really? If some freak took her brain, I doubted they were in a big hurry to bring it back.

"Karen, I'm not going to pretend to understand everything about your new school, but I don't think it's—Kyle! Keith! Don't you dare climb over that gate. You'll fall on your—hold on a second, hon." Mom let the phone clatter down onto a hard surface, making me wince and pull my cell a few inches away from my ear.

But even with the speaker at a distance, I could hear her yelling at my little brothers and sister. As if seventeen-month-old babies were going to listen to anything she had to say, no matter how scary her big bad mommy voice. That's the thing about babies, they're so … babyish, and determined to do exactly what they darn well please.

Not unlike myself.

I was determined to stay at school, no matter how scary it was to think about a human cranium harvester being loose in our midst. I wasn't going to be scared off by some psycho. That's giving in to terrorist tactics, or … something like that. Besides, I had a strange feeling I'd be able to help find Kendra's brain before it was too late. I'd always been good at solving puzzles, and my gut told me that I already had part of this one put together.

Gah! I wished my mom would hurry up and get back on the phone. I was dying to talk to Trish about the blood I'd seen on Gavin's shoes. I hated to suspect McDoMe, but blood-splattered Converse? *Highly* suspicious.

"I'm on hold." I rolled my eyes again. "The trips are acting up."

"So, is she freaking out?" Trish had called her mom a few minutes before and endured a major screamfest, but in the end her mom had said Trish could stay at school. Mostly because she was a single parent and wasn't home until six thirty and worried about Trish being alone at their apartment all day while she was at work.

"Not at bad as I thought. But yeah," I said, feeling strangely sad again.

When I was alive, there was no way Mom would have let me stay at a school where some girl had gotten her brain ripped out. I would have been whipped out of PHS and stuck in the private Catholic girls' school in Atlanta before I could formulate a decent whine about scratchy plaid skirts.

Though, man, what wouldn't I give *now* to be able to wear a Catholic schoolgirl outfit instead of my wretched robe? I'd stripped the atrocity off as soon as Trish and I got back to my room and was lounging in my brightest pair of Hello Kitty pajamas. Say what you will about my taste being juvenile, but I love the Kitty of the Hello.

And, as an added bonus, the friendly Kitty faces all over my pink pants seemed to drive Clarice into a near-catatonic state of despair. She'd sat and stared and drooled for a few minutes, then mumbled something about having a migraine and headed down the hall to her friend Darby's room. Now Trish and I could chill without the tragic sighs of psycho girl interrupting.

"Karen, you there?" Mom asked, completely out of breath.

Triplets will do that to you. That's why I *never* intended to reproduce. My mom got knocked up with triplets without any fertility treatments or anything. That meant having lots of babies at once was a hereditary thing for our family and … so … I …

"Karen? Hello?"

"Um, yeah. I'm here," I said, my voice trembling a bit. Death Challenged girls couldn't have kids. Our reproductive organs didn't function after death. I'd learned that today in Health.

Which was great since I wasn't going to miss having my period one single iota. But kids …

I mean, I'd just said I didn't want to reproduce. I guess it was knowing the choice wasn't mine to make anymore that made me a little sniffly.

"Honey, you don't sound good. You must be scared to death. Why don't I send Dad down to get you when he gets home from work? I would come now, but the van's on the fritz and I can't fit all three car seats in the—"

"No," I said, pulling myself together. Just last night I would have been thrilled to have my dad come pick me up, but that was before Trish. Now that I had a friend, DEAD was looking like a much better place to be.

My classes today had been pretty cool too. Even math wasn't as bad as it had been at my human school, and *Secrets of Successful Morticians and Their Uses for the Undead:*

Foundation and Beyond, my seventh period class, was positively amazing. Where else would makeup application be a mandatory class for all freshmen? I was really looking forward to learning how to use pancake foundation and cream rouge to look as human as possible when venturing out in the daylight without an illusion spell.

In order to learn that, and everything else I needed to know, I had to stay at DEAD.

"I'm fine, Mom. I promise. I'm not scared. Well, I am, a little. But I don't want to leave school."

"I know you don't, but—"

"I just got here, and I think it's important for me to stay." I was careful to use my big girl voice and not allow the hint of a whine to creep into my tone. Whining just made for a cranky, uncooperative Mom, and she already sounded pretty cranked out. "Besides, Principal Samedi has called in all kinds of extra security, and we're being careful to stay in pairs. My friend Trish is here in my room with me right now."

"You already made a friend? That's great, honey, I'm so glad you're—Kimberly Mae Vera! Put that down! Karen, can I call you back? I—"

"Fine, Mom, but I'm staying at school. It's settled, okay?"

"I'll have to talk to your father, but as long as there aren't any other— Kimmy! No!" The line went dead a second later. I snapped my cell closed with a sigh.

At this point, I was almost glad to be a Death Challenged weirdo who had been sent away to boarding school. I was only an hour away from my parents, so I could still see them on weekends—once I got a pass from Samedi and learned how to keep a basic illusion spell active—but I had the luxury of escaping the trips a large portion of the time. I loved those little monsters, but geez could they make life chaotic.

Though I supposed I should have preferred living in chaos rather than a place where a girl had lost her brain through foul play.

"So you're staying?" Trish smiled, her brown eyes lighting up.

She looked much fresher now, having chowed down on the raw cow-brain snack-pack the cafeteria had delivered to our rooms due to lunch period being interrupted by untimely death. It was almost good enough to make me glad I'd lost the chance to try out the hot line. Slimy and gross or not, raw brains really do things for a girl's complexion.

An Undead girl's complexion, anyway.

"Looks like it." I returned her grin and reached for the discarded pink nail polish, determined to add as much pink as possible to my body in order to annoy my sworn enemy, Clarice. "She said she's going to ask my dad, but I know he'll want me to stay. He took us on vacation to New York the summer after the September eleventh attack. He wanted to support the city and show we weren't going to be scared away by terrorists and all that."

"That's so cool. I've always wanted to go to New York."

I shrugged. "I was really little, so I don't remember it that well. And that was before the trips were born. Since then, we haven't gone anywhere. They're way too travel-unfriendly and expensive."

"Still, it must be nice having brothers and sisters. I always wanted a brother," Trish said, that wistful, only child look in her eye. I totally understood that look. I'd sported it myself until I was twelve.

"Yeah, it is nice," I admitted. "But it will be even nicer once they're potty trained. Three babies make a crapload of diapers."

We giggled a bit over that one. Diapers. Crapload. Ha!

But as soon as Trish reached for the white nail polish to start on the polka dots she had planned for her big toes, I knew it was time to get down to more serious matters than the standard new-BFF getting-to-know-you chatter and poop jokes.

"Okay, don't freak out, but I think I may have some evidence about the attack on Kendra." I dropped my voice to a whisper. More for dramatic effect than for fear anyone might hear—I mean, unless the cranium harvester was hiding out in my closet or something…

Hmm…just in case, I should probably…

"Evidence? In your closet?" Trish asked, shooting me a concerned look as I turned away from my totally murderer-free closet. Wow, paranoid much, Karen?

I tried to laugh off my weirdness as I climbed back onto the bed. "Nope, just checking to make sure I had a clean uniform for tomorrow." I hurried on before she could realize I'd only been at school one day and had been issued five uniforms and so surely had at least four clean ones left. (We were both bad at math, but not *that* bad.) "I'm talking blood splatters. When I leaned over in the lunch room, I saw that Gavin's shoes were covered in blood."

"Gavin? But there's no way he had anything to do with what happened to Kendra."

"Why? Because he's a hottie? Is there some rule that hot guys can't go psycho?"

"No, but ... he wouldn't do something like that," she said, her forehead bunching between her eyes. "He's a really great guy. He probably got the blood on his shoes while he was working in the cafeteria. They do all the butchering right here on campus. Principal Samedi uses the animal bones in a lot of her spells, so—"

"But doesn't he just work the entrance?" I asked, not willing to abandon my only clue so easily. "How would he get blood on his shoes if he never went back into the kitchen?"

"I don't know. Maybe he does do some work back there," Trish said, starting to sound angry. "I don't know how they break down the duties. I applied for a caf job, but they were all filled and freshmen were last on the waiting list. I got toilet duty instead." (Zombie bowels still work mostly the way human ones do. Odd, considering our hearts don't beat, but I guess all those brains have to go somewhere.)

"Ewww … I'm sorry. That's gross."

"Tell me about it. But we all have to do some kind of work on campus." Trish sighed, a melancholy sound that made me want to give her a hug. I totally would have, if my fingernails had been dry. "It's how we pay back the school for taking us in."

"Really?" I asked, wondering if I was going to be assigned some nasty job once I got settled in at DEAD. Not that I minded hard work, but cleaning a public toilet was not my idea of a good time. Heck, I didn't even like cleaning my own private toilet at home, and those were only *my* germs.

Ick! I was getting squicked out just thinking about the possibility of facing down a dorm lav with rubber gloves and industrial cleaner.

"Don't worry, you won't have to pull work detail," Trish said. Apparently my fears had shown on my face. "You're genetically Death Challenged. Only the Deprogrammed have to do work-study."

"Really?" I asked. Wow, shades of a John Hughes film. Trish was totally the poor girl who had to make her own clothes for the dance and I was the rich jerk who stole her boyfriend … or whatever that movie had been about. I'd only checked it out because it had "pink" in the title, but I'd fallen asleep halfway through. "That doesn't seem very fair."

"I don't know. If it hadn't been for Principal Samedi, I wouldn't have had the chance at another life. I would have been dead at fourteen and that's it." Trish smiled, obviously determined to put on her happy face. She would have been an excellent cheerleader. 'Twas a pity such a spirited grin was going to waste. "And it's not like all the DCs are jerks to the DPs or anything. Some of them are actually fairly decent people." She nudged me on the arm, and I grinned.

"Thanks, but…" My grin faded when I met Trish's eyes. A horrible realization pricked at the edge of my mind. "Is that why people have been looking at us funny? Do the Death Challenged and the Deprogrammed not usually—"

"No, not usually." Trish glanced down at her perfectly polka-dotted big toes.

"Wow. I thought it was because I was so short."

"Nope."

"And you were so tall," I added, not sure what to say.

"So, do you wish you'd drawn someone cooler as your first day tour guide? Someone born to be Undead?" Trish's expression was a little sad and a *lot* angry.

Which she had a complete right to be, but not at me.

"No way. I'm *so* glad I met you, and I was so happy when you asked me to sit with you at lunch," I rushed to assure her. "We have so much in common, I feel like we've been friends way more than a day and—"

"Even if the other DCs think you're strange?"

"Who cares what they think? *They're* strange if they

get all weird about how someone became Undead. I mean, we're basically all in the same boat. Right?" And here I'd thought people were so nice at DEAD. Guess they were nice if you were part of the in-crowd. What hoo-ha. I'd never been into that crap when I was alive (there were cheerleaders, drama girls, and band chicks at my old lunch table, and my best friend Piper was a volleyball player with a pathological aversion to skirts), and I certainly wasn't into it now. No one was going to tell me who I could or couldn't be friends with.

"Totally. And there are some DCs who think just like you," Trish said, though she looked even more depressed than before. "Though that might not be true for long."

"What do you mean?"

"There was a rumor going around earlier this year." Trish leaned close, her voice dropping to a whisper. A shiver worked down my spine, and the urge to check the closet for brain predators returned with a vengeance. "People were saying that Deprogrammed kids could become stronger and faster than DCs. That, with the right magic, we could be like superheroes compared to the genetically Undead. But only if we work this super-hard spell within the first two years of our deaths."

"Really?" I asked, the lame part of my brain glad I was befriending the Deprogrammed, just in case. As any good politician knows, it's never good to alienate a part of your constituency. Not that I really had a constituency... or planned on running for zombie office at any point in the near future, but yeah...

"Really. But this spell requires brains."

"Well, we've got lots of those hanging ar—"

"Not animal brains." Trish looked squicked, so I knew I wasn't going to like what she had to say next. "The brains of other Undead."

"Oh." My stomach cramped for the tenth time that day. "So whoever took Kendra's brain…"

"Might be one of us," Trish said, then flushed red. "I mean, one of me. The Deprogrammed."

"Superhero powers would be nice to have," I said slowly. "But nice enough to kill for?"

"I don't know." Trish's misery was as thick as brain jelly; I could practically taste it on my tongue. "But I bet that's what people are going to think. Being Deprogrammed will be even worse by tomorrow."

"But, wasn't Kendra Deprogrammed? I mean, if she had work-study, she would have to be, right?" I asked. Trish nodded. "So why would a Deprogrammed kid take the brains of another Deprogrammed kid? They could have taken any zombie's brains. It didn't have to be a DP's brains."

"I don't think so, no." Trish wrinkled her nose, deep in thought. "That doesn't really make sense, does it? I certainly wouldn't kill another Deprogrammed. Not that I would ever kill *anyone*! I'm just saying."

I laughed at her horrified expression. "I know. But it makes sense. Why kill another kid who's like you, when you could kill an annoying 'I'm so much better than you'

DC? Unless they plan on returning the brains? Does the spell—"

"No. I'm pretty sure the spell called for eating them. I think it said something about mixing a bunch of different brains in a pot and..." Trish swallowed hard, going as white as the dots upon her pink toes. "But I know it definitely called for a bunch of brains. Which means—"

"That while Kendra was the first, she won't be the last," I said, my voice sounding grimmer than I could ever remember.

But then, realizing there's one murder down and more to come is pretty grim stuff.

FIVE

The magic of the Death Challenged is, by its very nature, of the darkness and more easily lent to evil works than good. Therefore, it is a magic that should only be used sparingly, like butter upon a roll, not icing upon a cake.

—Introduction to Magical Behaviors,
Year One Syllabus

You could be my darkness,
you could be my soul,
you could be my zombie girl
wrapped in a blanket roll.
Zombie girl, oh yeah, yeah, zombie girl.

—"Zombie Girl," by the Resurrectionists, Sounds of
the Undead, 1940–1950

———————

Wednesday morning, the entire mood of the DEAD campus had shifted. Girls looked at each other suspiciously as they slunk into the bathroom for a morning shower and tooth brushing, the conversations at breakfast were hushed and tense, and there was much accusatory staring over scrambled brains toward the side of the room where the Deprogrammed were sitting. (And me, because

I was waiting for Trish, who didn't make it to breakfast. Of course! Therefore totally missing my show of solidarity.)

Now that I knew about the whole DC vs. DP controversy, the animosity between the two groups was abundantly clear. I couldn't believe I hadn't noticed something before. But then I am rather self-absorbed and I was getting used to an entirely new school, so I decided to cut myself some slack.

In the halls before class, things were even worse. Accusations flew from the bolder DCs, and two senior boys even got into a scuffle. Luckily, Gavin was there when the fists started to fly. He and a couple of swim-team pals pulled the two guys apart and convinced them to chill. Gavin was one of the few Deprogrammed on the swim team. Trish had told me that most DPs found they couldn't juggle work-study and sports practice, but he did, and he seemed well-liked by both the DPs and DCs.

Which kind of made me rethink him as a suspect. Why would a DP who was already so popular want to become a superhero?

But then, why *wouldn't* he want to become a superhero? Stronger, faster, and better was a good thing, no matter how popular you were. Right? And no matter how I tried, I couldn't seem to forget about the blood I'd seen on his shoes.

Unfortunately for me, suspecting a sex god of murder did not in any way lesson his effect upon my girlish sensibilities. When Gavin spotted me at my locker and came bounding over with a big grin on his face, I couldn't help but grin back. And giggle dorkily, and maybe drool a little bit. (Though I really hope I'm wrong about that last part.)

"Hey, Karen. How's it going?" The way he stared deep into my eyes made it feel like he really cared. This was no idle conversation—this was a meaningful inquiry into the state of my soul.

Sigh.

"A little freaked out. Trish told me about the whole Deprogrammed superhero spell thing," I said, trying to watch his expression for signs of guilt, but instead getting sucked into the gorgeousity that was McDoMe. Surely someone so beauteous couldn't be an evil brain thief.

"Oh, that." Gavin rolled his eyes. "That's the stupidest thing. Only a high priest or priestess could work that kind of magic, not some kid. That's what we told those two losers who were fighting."

"Yeah?" I wondered if this meant Gavin thought *I* was stupid for bringing up the spell in the first place. Crap! I knew I should have checked my facts before I started questioning potential suspects.

"I mean, a freshman wouldn't know that," he said with a comforting smile. Ahh ... McDoMe. It was like he could read my mind and was hurrying to allay my fears. Could he be any more perfect? Assuming he wasn't a cranium harvester, of course. "Seniors should know better. But maybe they slept through magical behaviors sophomore year."

"Maybe." I smiled back at him as I did my best to (1) remember my locker combination and (2) execute said combination with Gavin standing so close. "But it seems like a lot of people are seriously disturbed."

"And they should be. Some sicko harvested Kendra's brain." Wow, Gavin looked a lot meaner when he was angry, that was for sure. But he also looked even more unbearably yummy. Be still, my nonbeating heart. "Until they find out who did it, everyone should be careful. But I'm sure Principal Samedi will—hey, you dropped something."

He bent down and grabbed a piece of lavender paper that had fallen out of my locker, glancing at it before handing it over. While he glanced, I sneakily checked out his shoes. Black boots today, without a spec of blood splatter in sight. I was pretty relieved until I looked back up and saw that he was still perusing the paper.

I hurried to pluck it from between his fingers, praying it didn't say anything embarrassing. I didn't know anyone well enough for them to be leaving me shame-inducing notes, but a girl could never be too careful when she was the new kid.

"Thanks. And thanks for the information."

"No problem." Gavin smiled. "I'd better go. See you at lunch?"

"Yeah! See you," I said, tossing my ponytail.

You can take the girl out of the cheerleading squad, but you can't take the cheerleading squad out of the girl. My signature pony toss, once employed while thrusting my fist into the air and urging the Peachpit fans to give it up for their team, was still as perky and attention-getting as ever. I could have sworn Gavin looked over his shoulder *at least* twice before turning the corner at the end of the hall.

He was totally acting like he liked me! Gah, was I ever praying he wasn't the brain thief.

Unfortunately, I was so addled by our meeting and my crushy thoughts that I didn't look down at my note until the first bell rang.

> *Meet me in the girls' bathroom on the second floor before first period. I've got new evidence. Hugs, You know who. (I'm not going to sign this in case it falls into the wrong hands!)*

"Crap!" I grabbed my books and made a dash for the girls' room. Trish had obviously had more success investigating than I had.

Of course, she *did* know a lot more people. The only other person I was on chatting terms with was Clarice. Sort of. At least I talked *at* her and she occasionally threw an obscenity or two my way. Last night, I'd managed to freak out my freak-tastic roommate by asking a bunch of questions about who she thought might have it in for Kendra. In the end, I'd gotten nothing but the middle finger and some vague threat involving my bedspread and a package of black dye. No matter how pleasing it had been to spook the girl who seemed to enjoy nothing more than long, intimate conversations with her chicken bone collection, it was frustrating to go to bed without being any closer to the truth.

Which made me plenty eager to hear what Trish had found. I only had ten minutes before the tardy bell rang, and I didn't want to be late the first week—especially not to Cork's class—but I didn't want to stand Trish up, either. Especially since she'd still been bummed when she left my room last night.

I'd decided to risk tardiness and scary Cork be darned, but as I hustled up the stairs to the second floor, I smelled the telltale scent of my teacher's head-exploding cologne. I tried to hide behind my English book as we passed on the landing, but it was no use. The man had potentially tardy student radar or something.

"You've got three and one half minutes, Miss Vera. I anticipate you will be in class on time," he said, his pale gray eyes still glued to the folder in his hands. It was like he'd just *known* I was there. Creepy. But then that pretty much summed up Mr. Cork.

Yesterday, he'd suggested that my theme on "My first day as a member of the Undead" could be enhanced by describing the sensations I'd felt as my father scooped my brain back into my skull. Shudder. Morbid to the blechk degree. But then, what did I expect from a ghoulish-looking guy who'd been dead nearly three hundred years?

"I will," I assured him, trying to hold my breath until we'd passed each other, but still catching another headful of his signature stank. Ugh. Whoever had sold him that stuff should be dragged out into the street and shot—after being forced to inhale that heinous cologne for a few hours first. It really was rank. A single whiff of *eau de Cork* never failed to turn my stomach.

Of course, that could be said of many things lately. My Undead stomach was not nearly as iron-clad as my living one. Which made me wonder if they had a zombie version of Tums. If they did, I would have to start carrying some in my backpack.

"Now you have three minutes," Cork threw over his shoulder.

"I just need to use the restroom. Be right back." I took the last few stairs at a run and bolted for the door to the girls' bathroom like a zombie who'd broken the no-dairy rule (the results of which aren't pretty, according to my health book), already planning exactly what I'd say to Trish.

"Hey, I can only talk a second, so ... Trish?" My voice echoed off the tile walls of the eerily dark bathroom.

The small bulbs above the sinks were still on, but the overhead lights had been shattered. Glass littered the floor in front of the first two stalls and crunched lightly beneath my black boots as I moved deeper into the apparently deserted room.

"Um, hello? Is anyone in here?" More echoing ensued, and the strange hollowness of my own voice sent a chill skittering across my skin. This bathroom was even creepier than Cork, and obviously Trish-free. She must have decided to head to class when she heard the first bell ring.

I was turning around, prepared to follow her lead, when I saw them: a pair of brown loafers—approximately size 7 or 8 if my shoe-sense wasn't failing me—sticking out from under the doorway of the last stall. The toes were pointed straight toward the ceiling, which meant, whoever was in there, she was lying down on the germ-ridden bathroom floor.

Which also probably meant the chick in question was in a bad way, since no one in their right mind would *choose* to take a catnap on the floor of the lady's lav. She must have passed out or fallen down or something.

"Great," I muttered under my breath as I trudged toward the stall, hoping there wouldn't be any blood involved in whatever mishap had occurred. I don't do blood. Not even to be a Good Samaritan. If the girl was bleeding, I was so going to leave her there and run for help. There would be no looping a bloody arm in mine or leaning a crimson brow against my shoulder or anything of that nature.

Ew. Just thinking about the red stuff made me blecky, and my tummy was full-on rolling by the time I reached the door to the stall and gently pushed it open.

"Hello? Are you—ohmygod!" I screamed and scrambled backwards, gluing myself to the wall furthest from the mess on the floor.

That was all it was—a mess. I couldn't think of it as a person. And I especially couldn't think of it as a person who'd had their skull opened and their brain removed with the little garden trowel lying next to them on the tile.

"Ohmygod, ohmygod," I chanted in a trembling voice as I backed toward the door of the girls' room, my stomach heaving and my breath coming in desperate little pants.

Never in my entire life had I felt so close to passing out. Little gray spots danced around the edges of my eyes, and my head felt like it was going to swing around in a full circle and fall clean off my body, but I knew I *couldn't* let myself lose consciousness.

I couldn't pull a girly faint while still in the same room as a brain-harvest victim or I would completely lose my mind from fear. Or maybe even *literally* lose my mind if whoever had taken the girl's brain was still around, lurking in wait for another easy victim.

As if summoned by my terrified thoughts, the bathroom door swung open and, before I could turn around, heavy footsteps rushed me from behind. Something rock hard smashed down on the back of my head. The little gray dots turned into big black patches, which spread until I sank to the floor with a whimper, and the entire world went dark.

SIX

Dairy allergies are rampant among the Undead. Though some Death Challenged individuals may consume cow's milk without ill effect, the risk of severe allergic reaction—including shortness of breath, irritable bowels, seizures, paralysis, and even death—make it advisable to avoid milk and milk by-products.

—*Total Health for the Death Challenged, 5th Edition*

Zombie Joe lost his toe and still went a courtin',
Zombie Beth lost her breath, but still got up in the
    mornin',
But Zombie Fred lost his head and now we're all a
    mournin'
Mournin', mournin', we all fall down.

—*Traditional Irish Zombie folk song, late 18th century*

———————

I wasn't dead! I mean, I was still *dead,* as in, still a zombie, but I hadn't shuffled off my mortal coil. Still, if I didn't get something for the pain, the excessive pounding in my skull was going to make me wish I had. I couldn't remember anything hurting so bad, even my pavement dive the day I'd really died.

"Drugs," I groaned, smacking my dry lips. "I need drugs."

"Ohmygod! She's awake. Principal Samedi! Dr. Connor!" Trish's worried face appeared above me a second later. Her eyeliner had run at the edges and her brown eyes shone with more unshed tears, assuring me I looked as bad as I felt. "Karen, god, we were so worried. Are you okay?"

"Drugs..." I feebly moaned again, hoping someone would understand that I was talking pain relievers, not illegal contraband. I couldn't remember the name of the particular drug I was craving.

All my thoughts were muddy, foggy around the edges. I knew my name and age and shoe size and favorite shade of lipstick and all that, but for the life of me I couldn't remember what had—

"The bathroom!" It was coming back to me—the creepy bathroom, the blood on the floor, the scary footsteps rushing up behind me. "There was a girl...she was...someone had—"

"We know. The victim was discovered by the same hall monitor who found you unconscious on the floor." Principal Samedi appeared on my other side and took my hand in hers, applying pressure between my thumb and pointer finger. Amazingly, the pain rocketing through my skull began to fade. I mean, I still wanted drugs, but whatever hippie acupressure thing she was up to *did* help.

"It was Penelope Sweetney, another new freshman," Trish said, sniffling into a Kleenex that a grandmotherly looking person in a lab coat (Dr. Connor?) pressed into her hand. "She'd only been here three weeks, and now she's dead."

"She's not dead. We're going to find the person responsible in time to restore both Penelope and Kendra." Principal Samedi's sharp voice made me jump, and a fresh wave of agony slice through my head.

O drugs, sweet drugs, where were they when I needed them? Why had they forsaken me? Would this Dr. Connor—who was cranking up the top of my bed until I was in a seated position—give me something for the pain if I asked? Or was I destined to suffer for all eternity, doomed to live out the rest of my Undeath with a killer migraine?

Guess that was better than *not* living *without* my brains, but—

"My brain!" I shouted, panic in my voice. "It's still there, right? I mean, he didn't take it, didn't harvest it or whatever?"

"He? Are you sure it was a man who attacked you?" Samedi's face was scary intense, and the fingers digging between my finger and thumb began to hurt. "Did you get a good look at him? Can you give a description to—"

"Hold on a second, Theresa," Dr. Connor said. "Let's give Karen a chance to get her bearings." Smoothly, the doc moved closer to the bed, brushing Principal Samedi aside. "Bet you've got quite a headache, don't you, sweetie?" I nodded, almost teary with relief. "Just try to hold still while I finish the examination, and then we'll get you something to make you feel much better."

"Examination? To make sure my brain is still there?" I did my best to suck the tears filling my eyes back inside my sockets. The logical part of me insisted my brains *had* to be okay or I wouldn't be able to *ask* about them, but I couldn't keep from stressing.

Before this week, the grossest thing I'd ever seen had been the fake autopsy victim at the Jaycee's annual haunted house—or the trips' nursery the day all three of them had the flu and projectile baby vomited at the same time. Blechk. *The Exorcist* chick had nothing on those three when it came to spew. It'd looked like a curdled milk factory had exploded and smelled even worse.

Oh god, now I felt like I was going to be sick. Why did I have to dwell on spew? Why?

"Your brain is fine. You've just got a nasty dent in your skull." Dr. Connor patted the hair around said dent softly, her gentle touch reminding me of my mom's, which made me even more sniffly. "But it's nothing a good meal won't cure. I'll have something sent up from the cafeteria." She turned back to Principal Samedi with a stern look. "You can ask your questions, but keep it brief."

Principal Samedi nodded meekly as Dr. Connor headed out of the room, presumably to order up a big mess of raw brains. "She's my great-great grandmother," Samedi confided with a smile as she resumed her death grip on my hand. It didn't feel good anymore, but I was reluctant to say anything about it. Nice lady or not, Principal Samedi still gave me a mild case of the creeps. "Even principals need someone to keep them in line."

I smiled and tried to ignore the strange look on Trish's face. My new BFF was standing a bit behind our fearless leader so Samedi couldn't see the panic and suspicion in her eyes, but I could. Trish was afraid of more than whoever was harvesting brains at DEAD—she was afraid of Principal Samedi.

But why? I mean, yes, Samedi was a little creepy, but she was basically good people. Wasn't she? Trish had seemed to like her before. But maybe something had happened while I was unconscious. For all I knew, Samedi could have said she hated blond former cheerleaders and begged Clarice to cut off my head while I slept.

Argh! I was dying to jump off the bed and pull Trish back to my room for some serious debriefing, but for now I was stuck.

"Do you feel up to answering a few questions?" Samedi asked. "If not, I can always find you later in the day. I don't want—"

"No, I'm fine. I'll tell you everything I remember, but…it isn't much." I briefly recounted my tale of woe, from the moment I stepped into the girls' room and saw the body, to the sound of the heavy footsteps, to the whack on my head and the world fading to black.

"So, you didn't get a look at your attacker? Couldn't say if it was a male or a female?" Samedi looked suspiciously pleased by this news. Why would she be *glad* to be no closer to identifying her perp?

"No. I just thought it was probably a man because of

the shoes. They sounded big, with a thick sole, like something a guy would wear."

"And it definitely could be. We're not going to rule that out." She stepped back, putting an arm around Trish in a gesture that should have looked motherly and sweet, but didn't. Principal Samedi just wasn't the maternal type; she was too cool and collected, not nearly messy enough for the mom gig. "But from the depth of your wound, we were thinking you'd been hit by a female or an adolescent male."

"Couldn't it have been a grown man who just didn't use all his strength?" I asked.

"Possibly," Principal Samedi said, but I could tell she wasn't buying that theory. "Or he could have been in a hurry. We believe whoever it was fled the bathroom not long after striking you. The hall monitor said she heard something drop to the ground outside the bathroom window."

"But she didn't see anything?"

"Unfortunately, no. Still, you're very lucky she came along when she did."

I tried to nod, but stopped when a head twinge reminded me of my injury. "I guess I owe her my brain."

Principal Samedi smiled grimly while Trish made a face that looked like she'd been forced to eat live insects. What was up with her? I wish I'd known her longer. If she were my old best friend, Piper, I'd know exactly what her weird facial expressions meant.

Piper. Sniff. I missed her and my old life. A lot.

I've never been one to dwell on the past or what could have been, but this whole Undead thing was turning out way scarier than I'd thought it would be. It made me wistful for the days when I'd assumed learning to eat raw pig brains was the absolute worst thing I'd have to deal with here at DEAD.

"I've got to get back to organizing the enhanced security, but Trish will stay with you until you're feeling better." Principal Samedi released her snuggle captive and strode purposefully toward the door to the infirmary. "I'll see you both sixth period."

Trish and I had Samedi for *Introduction to Magical Behaviors*, a class that, so far, wasn't nearly as fun as it sounded. It was mostly a bunch of rules and lectures on why we should never even attempt to harness the paranormal power we inherently possessed as the living dead except to work the illusion spells necessary for us to move around in the human world without being discovered. It was like a semester-long sex-ed class focused solely on abstinence. Logical and safe, maybe. But very, very boring. We should at least get to put condoms on bananas ... or the magical behaviors equivalent.

"See you later," I said with a weak wave.

"Bye," Trish echoed, sidling closer to my bed. She waited until Samedi's footsteps faded down the hall before turning to clutch at my hand. "Are you really okay? Is that really what happened?"

"Yeah, except for the note." I'd left out the part about being summoned to the bathroom by Trish's note, not wanting to get my new friend in trouble. "I didn't think I should mention that part."

"Thank god you didn't," she said, keeping her voice to a whisper, as if she feared someone might be listening even though we were alone in the room. "Principal Samedi is lying."

"About what?"

"About everything! I snagged a pass and was on my way to the bathroom to check and see if you were still there waiting for me when the hall monitor found you. Renee came running out, saying she'd seen someone in a white robe go through the window, but it was like she forgot all about that after Principal Samedi pulled her aside."

A funny feeling skittered across my skin, raising all the little hairs on my arms. "You think Samedi brainwashed her or something?"

"Who knows?" Trish shivered, catching my chill. "But she's a high priestess and casts real spells on a regular basis. She'd probably know how to."

"I guess." I didn't know much about magic yet, but it did seem weird that while our principal was an out-of-the-closet caster who used leftover bones from the cafeteria to work magic, she urged all her students to never dabble in the art. Was she really trying to keep us safe or did she just want to keep the power all to herself? "A white robe would mean a teacher, right? Do you think she's trying to cover up the fact that a teacher whacked me on the head and stole Penelope's brains?"

"Maybe. I don't know. All I know is that she really, really creeped me out when—"

"Karen, are you okay?"

"Ahhh!!" Trish and I screamed and jumped about a foot in the air at the sound of the voice in the doorway.

I clutched my skull and groaned as my head reminded me how much it still hurt. Neither jumping nor screaming were good ideas for me right now. Geez! Where were my brains already? If they were going to deny me acetaminophen, it seemed the least they could do was put a rush on the raw gray matter.

"Sorry, didn't mean to scare you. I offered to bring up your food when I heard you'd been hurt." Gavin stood in the doorway, looking as delicious as ever, holding a cafeteria tray covered with a silver lid. "I wanted to make sure you were all right."

"Oh. Thanks. That's great!" I said, wincing at the girly excitement in my own voice. Only a chick with a horrible crush could sound so perky after being attacked in the toilet. Could I be more embarrassingly eager?

Thankfully, Gavin didn't seem to notice. He just smiled that dimple-popping smile. "So, is it all right if I come in?"

"Sure, yeah, come in." I sat up a little straighter, wishing I'd had the chance to glance in a mirror since coming to. I couldn't be certain, but I was guessing "head recently bashed in" wasn't a good look for me. If only I'd gotten my hands on some lip-gloss before it was too late!

But Gavin didn't seem to notice my drab factor, either.

In fact, he couldn't take his eyes off of me as I opened my get-well meal and started shoveling in the brains as fast as was moderately ladylike. I couldn't take my eyes off of him, either. He was just so...yummy. Crazy yummy. Maybe even dangerously yummy.

If Trish hadn't made a strangled-stork sound and jerked her thumb several times toward Gavin's clothes, I don't know if I ever would have pulled myself out of the tractor beam of his eyes in time to take note of his *second* uniform violation in two days.

"Um, so, what's with the outfit?" I asked as casually as I could, considering I had a mouthful of brains and a head full of suspicion. There Gavin stood in a glaringly *white* robe! "Do juniors get special privileges or something? If so, I can't wait. I'm so over the all-black look."

Gavin laughed with apparent innocence. "You'll have to join the swim team, then. This is our meet robe. Principal Samedi says it's bad luck to wear black on a competition day. Not that it really matters." His smile faded. "The meet's been cancelled. Everything except classes has been cancelled until they find this psycho. They're sure whoever did this will kill again. It's only a matter of time."

"Is it?" I asked, arching my recently plucked brow. At least I hadn't let that grooming task slip. I might presently be lip-glossless, but I knew that the "frames of my face" were in excellent condition.

"Yeah...I think so." Gavin met my challenging look with one of his own. For a second I could have sworn he was accusing *me* of something before his hottie mask fell back into place. "But I've got to get back to class. Take care, you two."

"We will. Don't worry," I called after him, meeting Trish's eyes over a huge drink of some sort of brain smoothie that had come with my meal.

And we would take care, oh yes, we would. Take care of *him* before he harvested another brain.

SEVEN

Smooth a bit of foundation onto your arm and blend, checking to make sure you've got a good match. Undead flesh will continue to grow considerably paler after death, so you may need to change foundations several times in your first few years as a Death Challenged individual. Remember, in order to hide in plain sight, the Undead must do their part. Cosmetics are your friends and allies, as much as any trick of magic.

—*Secrets of Successful Morticians and Their Uses for the Undead: Foundation and Beyond*

No way! She didn't! I hastily scribbled the words onto my notepad before shoving it into Trish's hands and waiting the eternity it took for her to write back in her best penmanship. We'd finished our homework for seventh period ages ago—I was no makeup virgin and had my exact foundation match and Trish's figured out in mere minutes—and so I had nothing to distract me while I waited.

It was so frustrating! Frustrating enough that I'd been willing to put up with the heat in Trish's room (she was lucky to have a single, although it was right next to the boiler room). But since she'd needed a break from the swelteringness, we'd stuck it out in my room.

Argh! This would be so much faster if we could have IMed, but the computers in our rooms weren't Internet equipped for some evil, twisted reason. Probably because the boys had been downloading naughty pictures or something lame, and now we all had to suffer. What was it with teachers and group suffering?

Speaking of suffering, if my roommate weren't so *in*sufferable, Trish and I could have just talked this thing out. But Clarice was being a complete investigation-killer, insisting she needed quiet time to commune with her chicken bone collection or whatever she was up to on the other side of the room, hiding under her thick black blanket with *my* Hello Kitty flashlight.

It seemed pink cuteness wasn't so intolerable when it came to something she needed. I suppose my belongings no longer had girlie cooties, either, since she'd lifted both my flashlight and two of my scrunchies before disappearing into her blanket lair seconds after I returned to our room.

I was trying to be cool with the "borrowing without asking" stuff, since we had been getting along a little bit better today. It would be best for both of us if we could stop annoying the hell out of each other. But if she laid a hand on my lavender-filled eye pillow, all bets were off. Thank god my feet were too small for her to even think about touching my shoes, or I doubt I would have slept until I'd purchased a lockbox.

She totally did. I swear I saw her touch your head and then lick the blood off her fingers. Like she was tasting you! Like you were a snack food!!! I almost barfed, but held it in so she wouldn't know I'd seen anything. I didn't want to get the Samedi mind wipe like Renee.

Ew!! So gross!! I held up the pad so Trish could nod her enthusiastic agreement, then let it drop back into my lap.

I couldn't believe Principal Samedi had *tasted* my blood. Blerchk! It was beyond squicky. Still, I just couldn't see her as the brain harvester. I knew this opinion was bugging Trish, so I chose my next words carefully.

Okay, so Samedi goes on the suspect list, for sure. Along with Gavin, other members of the swim team who had first period free, and any teachers who weren't present and accounted for during the minutes between eight o'clock and eight fifteen.

It was going to be a long list, but it was too soon to rule anyone out … though I knew who I was betting on, and it *wasn't* my bloodthirsty new principal.

Trish jabbed me with her bony elbow to get my attention and pointed emphatically at what she'd written.

She goes at the top of the list!

Okay … but what about my brain? We had to stop and have a brief giggle about that. It was just funny for some reason, but then Clarice grunted beneath her blanket of death and we did our best to quiet down. **I've been thinking and it seems weird that whoever hit me didn't try to harvest**

my brain. Assuming the person who attacked me was the same person who attacked Penelope, which it had to be or why else would they knock me out?

> Well, they could have been meaning to take yours too. How can we know they didn't just get interrupted?

They were already on their way out of the bathroom when Renee came in. That means they weren't trying to stick around and snatch my gray matter, or she would have seen them kneeling next to me, not running for the window.

> Hmm ... makes sense.

So why shun my brains?

Maybe they heard Renee coming? Or maybe ... Trish's pencil hovered above the paper while she chewed thoughtfully on her bottom lip. You know, both Penelope and Kendra were Deprogrammed ...

Dude, Trish was so good at this. I hadn't even remembered the whole Deprogrammed vs. Death Challenge controversy, but I should have. I blamed my head injury for not considering that angle from the get-go. So you think whoever did this left me alone because I'm naturally Death Challenged?

> Could be. Which would mean Gavin is innocent. Why would he attack his own kind but leave you with nothing more than a bump on the head?

Because he is crushing on me big time? In a psycho-killer-who-likes-to-steal-brains kind of way? Even though Gavin was my top suspect—due to his blood-splattered shoes, white robe, and the fact that he had totally seen the note Trish left in my locker and could have followed me to the bathroom—I couldn't help but be vaguely thrilled by this idea.

Trish rolled her eyes. *You are so vain.*

Am not!! Why did everyone try to crush my healthy self-esteem? Would the world only be satisfied when I spent hours staring at *US Weekly* and bemoaning the size of my thighs compared to the anorexic starlet of the moment?

Are too, you probably think this note is about you.

Um, it is.

I was joking. It's a line from an old song my grandmother likes. You really need to expand your knowledge of classic rock.

You mean grandmother music?

Classic! It's classic!! That means it will be cool forever! Trish stuck out her tongue, and we both giggled.

Clarice started making cow-going-into-labor moaning sounds under her blanket in response, but that only made it harder to stifle our mirth. She was *so* weird. I was totally going to see if I could apply for a room transfer before the start of next semester. I'd heard that, occasionally, Samedi would let three girls share the larger corner dorm rooms if there weren't any other spaces available. I didn't know the girls in those rooms very well yet, but *anyone* would be a better personality fit than Clarice the Tragic and Strange.

I put it on my mental to-do list: start kissing up to the girls with the larger rooms ASAP. Maybe I could make them some caramelized brain blondies if I could get transferred from *Zombie Internet Technologies* to *The Undead Hearth and Home* for third period. The technology class had more boys in it, which was nice, but I really needed to learn how to cook zombie food. Especially zombie desserts. Since chocolate had been removed from my diet, I'd been jonesing for sweet stuff big time. Besides, boys would come and go; dessert was forever.

Trish slid the notepad onto my lap. *But whatever, I still can't believe you even suspect Gavin. He is 2 cute 2B evil.*

Pretty is as pretty does. There's a little wisdom from my grandmother.

Who was very, very wise. She was the only person in my family who hadn't been completely taken in by my little sister, Kimmy, who is easily the most beautiful child in the world, but also the most evil. Well, not *evil.* "Mischievous" would be a better word, but I bet my brothers thought she was evil. The poor boys were endlessly tortured by their female third. For someone who hadn't reached her second birthday, Kimmy had a lot of naughty tricks up her pink onesie.

I got a little sad again, wishing I could go downstairs to the playroom and play with the trips before dinner. I missed those little turds, which just went to show how very serious my head injury had been. I should probably be lying down and avoiding all brain activity until I was healed, but this mystery was not going to solve itself.

It didn't look like Principal Samedi was doing much of anything to track down the harvester. Aside from a few extra uniformed guards patrolling the halls, I couldn't see any signs of an active investigation. Aside from our own, of course.

Back to Samedi. It's weird that she didn't make me call my parents to tell them what happened today. I'd been worried because I knew Mom and Dad wouldn't let me stay after being attacked by a psycho in the girls' lav, but Samedi had dismissed my concerns with a shrug and a vague "what they don't know" after sixth period. She'd said she didn't want to lose a new student over something that would be resolved in a day's time. Still, it made me wonder … I wasn't expecting her to agree to keep this under wraps.

She agreed because she is guilty and wicked … and probably doesn't want to get sued. Your parents seem like the suing type.

You've never even met my parents.

That's just the vibe I get, don't get upset. My mom would sue too, if she had the money to hire a lawyer. And if I was the one who'd had my head bashed in and the principal licking my yummy blood.

Ew!!! We started laughing again.

I don't know why, since it really wasn't funny. But when does laughter ever make sense? That's why comedy is so much harder to pull off than tragedy. I mean, a *lot* of things will make a *lot* of people cry, but everyone has a unique and particular sense of humor.

Except Clarice, who obviously had no sense of humor at all.

"Oh my god!! Could you just shut up already?" My roomate's pinched face emerged from beneath her blanket, her black hair a wild, greasy tangle and her cheeks bright red. "I'm trying to concentrate!"

"Should you really be using god's name in vain? Shouldn't you be calling upon the dark lord or something like that?" Trish asked, in this innocent voice that did nothing to conceal her smartass factor.

Trish had gotten a lot gutsier in the two days I'd known her. Criminal investigation clearly agreed with her. She should think about a career in law enforcement after we graduated. We needed good people out there protecting and serving, and she could always work the night shift so no one noticed her inhuman pallor. Or maybe she could work an illusion spell and be able to get her cop on during the day ... I wasn't sure how long an illusion spell could last.

I wasn't sure of anything where my new magic was concerned, which made me even more suspicious of Principal Samedi. Why was she so determined to keep all of her students ignorant of their potential? This was supposed to be a *learning* institution, after all.

"Shouldn't you be off scrubbing a toilet?" Clarice smiled, a nasty little twist of her lips that showcased her overbite. I had three words for this chick: Braces. With. Headgear.

Actually, I had more words for her than that, but Trish beat me to it.

"I guess I got distracted by the human stain living on your side of the room."

"You're the only stain I see, Trisha."

"Did anyone ever tell you those chicken bones smell even worse than your breath, Clarice?" Oh! That one hit home, you could tell. Clarice *did* have bad breath. Like, unusually bad. Maybe it had something to do with the overbite. I didn't know, but she was certainly hacked off at Trish now, no doubt about that. She threw off her blanket and jumped to her feet.

"You don't want to start with me, Trisha. I'm not the sort of enemy you can afford to make."

Trish stood up, easily towering over the much shorter Clarice, even in her sock feet. "Are you threatening me?"

"Maybe you're not as stupid as you look."

"Bullying is against school policy, Clarice. You'd know that if you spent less time hiding under your blanket with your freak collection."

"School policy? You're quoting school policy? That is, like, clinically dorky."

Clinically dorky? What exactly did *that* mean? A dork raised in a clinic? Clarice was losing her edge and her cool. She looked about ten seconds away from decking Trish. I had to get the situation under control before one or both of them got hurt. Whether she was a creepy chicken bone collector or not, I still had to live with Clarice for at least two more months, and I really didn't want Trish to get her so mad she decided to clip her toenails in my bed or something totally heinous.

"Listen, ya'll. Let's just calm down. There's no reason to—"

"Ya'll? Did you really just say ya'll?" Clarice turned on me with a snarl, spittle flying from the stank hole she called a mouth. Ew, the breath was worse than ever. Had she brushed her teeth this *year*? "What is your malfunction?"

"Last time I checked, this was Georgia," I said, unable to keep a bit of haughty from my tone. "'Ya'll' is the standard and preferred pronoun of our region when referring to—"

"You don't even know what a pronoun is, you stupid, pink…cheerleader! God!" Clarice was in tears by the time she ran from the room. What was with this girl? She was either screaming at me or bawling her eyes out. I was beginning to think she had a disorder of some kind, or at the very least needed some serious therapy.

Which made me wonder—did zombies have therapists? I'd have to ask my health teacher tomorrow.

"Did she just insult you by calling you pink?" Trish asked, sounding as baffled as I felt.

"A pink cheerleader," I mumbled, crossing to the door to peek into the hall. But Clarice had already disappeared. Probably gone to the girls' room to plot my and Trish's death.

"She is seriously disturbed," Trish said. "No wonder all her roommates moved out."

"All her roommates? How many has she had?"

"Five, I think. Three last year when we were in eighth grade, and then Libby was in here before you came. She just got a transfer like three days before you started class."

"Great, now you tell me," I moaned. This was so not fair! What had I done to deserve the freakiest roommate on the entire DEAD campus? Was it not enough that I'd been knocked unconscious my first week of school? "You're so lucky that you have a single, even if it is a sweat-hole. This whole Clarice situation just keeps getting worse."

"Sorry, K. I don't want to freak you out, but Darby's the only one who will have anything to do with Clarice, and that's only because they both practice magic."

I turned back to Trish, a scary new theory burbling to the forefront of my brain. "She practices magic, even though Principal Samedi tells us not to?"

"Well, it's not like forbidden or anything, so Samedi can't really stop Clarice or anyone else from trying to learn the voodoo stuff, but..." Trish collapsed back onto my bed, clutching my smiley face–shaped pillow and chewing on her lip. This was the thinking look, I realized, cheered by the knowledge that I was learning Trish's faces.

"But what?" I prodded when the thinking went on for too long.

"Samedi's never been too happy about it. I think she'd like to see Clarice leave DEAD, but Clarice has nowhere else to go. She's naturally Death Challenged, but her entire family died in the car wreck that made her that way."

"Oh wow, that's awful." Now I felt really bad about loathing Clarice. I would have to try to reach out to her again, see if we could start over and at least be civil if we couldn't be friends. That was assuming, of course, that she wasn't the brain harvester.

"It is, but so is she. It's hard to feel sorry for her, you know?"

I nodded. "Especially if she's the one out for brains. I mean, she's not a DP so she wouldn't be working the superpowers spell, but brains would give her own spells a lot more power than chicken bones, right?"

"They would," Trish agreed.

"Sounds like we need to find out where Clarice was this morning."

"Totally, but we should be careful not to jump to conclusions. What if Samedi is framing Clarice for the brain snatching in order to get rid of her?" Trish's eye went wide, and I could tell she was really digging this latest theory. "That would explain why she was so insistent on the person who hit you being a woman or a younger guy."

"True." I still wasn't on the "Samedi is guilty" crazy train, but I couldn't deny there had been something fishy about her behavior in the infirmary. "Before we rule out anyone, we need to find out who was where."

"And when," Trish agreed with a nod. "We should start with Clarice and the swim team since there will be a written record of whether any of them were absent or tardy or had first period free."

"Sounds good."

"So, when do we break into Samedi's office? Tonight or early tomorrow morning?"

Wow. I'd thought I would have to do some convincing to get Trish on the breaking-and-entering bandwagon. Maybe I'd been wrong about her having a future in law enforcement—she might be destined for a career on the wrong side of the law instead. Which could also be cool, as long as she didn't kill people and limited her criminal activities to stealing from evil corporations who damaged the planet and made kids work in sweatshops and stuff like that.

I'm of the opinion that some criminal activity is fine, as long as it's for a good cause and doesn't hurt innocent people. My mom says that makes me a sociopath and gives her a borderline case of the creeps, but I'm standing by my beliefs. Sometimes crime *does* pay, like when it helps you track down a brain harvester before anyone else is killed.

"I say tonight."

"Perfect." Trish grinned, obviously looking forward to

our fieldtrip as much as I was. "I'll meet you by the water fountains at the end of the hall at midnight."

"Midnight."

EIGHT

Secret messages from the High Council of the United States to the U.S. Undead community are encoded in the html of our national website: www.usofficeworkersunitingforalessbraindead workspace.com.

Simply go the homepage and click "view source." Then, follow the decoding directions in the back of your manual. The first two paragraphs will be due next Thursday.

—*Zombie Internet Technologies, Homework Directions*

"Could you hurry, please?" Trish hissed, wavering unsteadily beneath me like she was lifting a grown man with a donut-binging problem, not a former flyer for the PHS JV cheerleading team.

I barely weighed a hundred pounds, for god's sakes. She was being a total wimp, as well as shattering my belief that she would have been a valuable contributor to a spirit squad in her former life.

"You're crushing my spine."

"I am not!" I whispered, pushing up on one square of the ceiling and moving it out of the way.

Seeing as how we weren't seasoned criminals—yet—the office lock had been totally unpickable. So we'd decided crawling through the ceiling was the only way in. As the smaller partner in crime, I'd been charged with the crawling.

"You are too!" she groaned. "I think I heard something crack near my fifth vertebrae. I may never walk again."

I rolled my eyes and did my best not to think about how hard the tile floor beneath us truly was. If I took a dive off all five foot ten of Trish, I was going to re-dent my recently healed head and have a lot of explaining to do tomorrow morning at breakfast.

"So…heavy!" Trish gasped for breath and began to tremble in earnest.

"Just stand up a little straighter," I urged, forcing away flashbacks of my cheer-pyramid tragedy and wondering if I was too young to suffer from post-traumatic stress. "I can't reach."

"This is as straight as I stand with my spine crushed," Trish grumbled, but did manage to stretch her wimpy beanpole self up a few more centimeters.

I grabbed at the edge of the hole I'd made and flexed my muscles, never more grateful for the fact that I'd lifted weights in my former life. Not only did my little muscles give my arms great tone in a tank top, but once I'd hooked my right leg beside my hands, I had the strength to pull myself up and into the ceiling.

"Okay, throw me the rope." I turned around and reached out.

"Just give me a second." Trish bent double, panting. "You are *so* much heavier than you look."

"Muscle weighs more than fat."

"I think your bones are made of lead and you ate too much dinner."

"I think you're wimpy and need to get to the gym," I said. "And you need to hurry and throw me that rope. The guards could come back any second."

When we'd first snuck down the long hallway that connected the girls' dorm to the main school building, we'd seen several guards lingering near the office. Lucky for us, they'd gotten some sort of message on their walkie-talkie thingies and run off to another part of campus, but we couldn't afford to dawdle.

"Okay, fine." Trish grabbed the rope and, by the fourth or fifth try, managed to throw it high enough for me to reach.

"All right. I'm going in," I whispered, smiling at Trish's thumbs-up before I replaced the ceiling square, turned, and started the crawl.

It wasn't nearly as gross up in the ceiling as I'd thought it would be, which made me feel a whole lot better about being the designated crawler. Not to be totally girlie, but I'm not big on bugs or spiders or cobwebs or massive amounts of dust or dead bodies that have been wrapped in plastic and allowed to putrefy. (We were at a zombie school; I had no idea what to expect.)

After ten or twelve feet, I popped out another square of ceiling and peered down. Score. We were in. Now I just had to find something to tie my rope around. I needed some way to climb back out of the office if I couldn't get the door open from the inside.

Hmm … the choices were limited, but in the end I decided on a sturdy-looking pipe. Despite Trish's theatrics, I didn't weigh *that* much. The chances that I'd break the pipe and flood the office with water were fairly small. At least small enough for me to risk pipe damage in the name of solid investigative work.

Within a few minutes, I was dropping my rope down into the office and lowering myself over the edge. Unfortunately, I'd neglected to think about the rope burn factor. Even with my foot hooked around the rope for extra support, I still had bright red, throbbing palms by the time I reached the floor.

"Ouch, ouch, ouch." Crap. I'd just *ruined* my chances of climbing back out the way I'd come in. Which meant there would be no way to conceal the fact that *someone* had been sneaking into Samedi's office.

Argh! This was so not good! By tomorrow morning, Samedi and her crew would be wise to the fact that their inner sanctum had been breached. Now I could only pray they didn't have the ability to dust for fingerprints on the ceiling or match my DNA to the skin cells clinging to the rope. In a normal school, I wouldn't even think about something like that, but here at DEAD I wasn't so sure. Principal Samedi could have a forensic team on staff, for all I knew.

Though … it would seem she would have had Penelope and Kendra's bodies searched for prints if that was the case …

"Did they find any fingerprints on Penelope or Kendra? Did you hear anything about Samedi even looking for prints?" I asked, as I opened the door and let Trish inside. Turns out the lock was a simple dead bolt, nothing fancy, which meant the rope was a total waste.

So far, a criminal mastermind I was not.

"No, I didn't hear anything about prints, but Principal Samedi probably wouldn't go there. She's more of a magic person than a science person." Trish closed the door, then rushed to the registrar's desk at the back of the room and turned on the computer. "She'd probably work a spell to see who'd touched the body *if* she were really trying to figure out who was behind this."

"Could she work a spell to find out who climbed down that rope?" I asked, starting to get anxious. "I scraped my hands so there's no way I'm going to be able to climb back up and hide it."

"No worries." Trish dragged a chair over to the hole in the ceiling, turned an empty trashcan upside down on top, and then climbed up and tucked the rope back inside the ceiling. A second later, she'd tugged the tile back into place. I felt really, really dumb.

"Why didn't I think of that?" I asked, beginning to doubt my own intelligence. Maybe the whole dead thing had caused my IQ to plummet.

"Because you're short and don't have practice with these sorts of things."

"And you do?" I snorted, as Trish sat down behind the desk and took control of the mouse. She had aced *Zombie*

Internet Technologies last year and was great with computers, so we'd decided she should take point with the computer stuff.

"I spent a couple months in a juvenile detention center when I was twelve. I learned a lot of little tricks while I was there, but I knew my share before I went in."

"What?" Oh. My. God. I was hanging out with a criminal! I backed away from the desk, possessed by the sudden urge to turn and run back to my room. Sure, I'd been cool with *imagining* Trish's future as a crime lord, but faced with the actual reality of a BFF who'd done time, I wasn't so sure.

"Relax. It's not like I murdered someone or something. I got caught shoplifting one too many times, and my mom thought it would teach me a lesson to go to juvie, so she didn't fight the sentence." Trish shrugged, her attention focused on the screen in front of her. "And it did teach me a lesson. It taught me not to get caught."

"Yeah." Play it cool, just play it cool, Karen. You can hang with the criminal element. Blechk, who was I kidding? I was the least criminal person I knew! At least until tonight. "Not getting caught is good."

Trish sighed. "The shoplifting thing was just a stage I went through after my dad left. I'm totally over it now." Her gaze slid toward me, and for a second I saw the fear that I would judge her and not be her friend anymore in her eyes. "You know?"

"It's cool. I understand." And … I did.

After all, who was to say I wouldn't have done the same thing in her place? If my dad had left Mom and me and the trips and run off with some girl six years older than me, never to be heard from again, maybe I would have started stealing too.

More likely I would have run away, because my mother would have been declared mentally unfit to parent due to the stress of caring for three infants all by herself and a social worker would have come to try to place me and the trips in foster care. But that was beside the point. The point was, Trish and I *were* cool.

"Good." She smiled, but her grin faded as she turned back to the screen. "But this is *not* so good."

"What?"

"The entire swim team was out first period. Looks like they didn't have to report to class because of the meet or something."

"Crap!" That meant our suspect list hadn't been narrowed the slightest bit. All the breaking and entering had been for naught! Unless... "What about Clarice? I know she has a class first period. *Religions of the Dead and Undead*, I think. Was she there?"

"Looks like... she was..." Trish clicked a few more times. "*Not* there. At least not for the first part of class. She was marked tardy, and check this out."

I leaned down to look at where she'd pointed. "Darby was tardy too. That's—"

"Very suspicious." Trish's lips pressed into a thin line

as she shut down the computer and wiped the keyboard with the edge of her sleeve. Looks like she was taking my fingerprint worry to heart, no matter what she'd said about Samedi preferring magic over science.

"Very. Do you think they were off harvesting brains together? Maybe they're saving them up for some sort of magic?"

"Could be," Trish said. "Darby is Deprogrammed, so she could be trying to work that spell everyone's been talking about, the one that would make her into a super zombie."

"But why would Clarice be helping her with that? What's in it for her?"

"A super BFF? Maybe she's just so desperate for friends that she—"

We both heard it at the same time, the metallic click as the door handle turned, followed by creaking as it swung open on its hinges. The filing cabinet in front of us offered a few seconds of cover, but we were going to have to find a place to hide. Fast!

Trish dove under the desk and, after a second's hesitation, I followed. It was going to be a tight fit under there, but there just wasn't anywhere else to go. Trish's eyes bulged as I crammed in beside her, but she didn't say a word, even when I accidentally clocked her in the nose with my knee. (Don't ask, it was really crowded under there. I don't know how my knee got that close to her nose, it just did.)

Heavy footsteps sounded on the tile floor, each one landing with a horrible, echo-less finality that heralded my and Trish's impending doom. I squeezed my eyes shut as they got closer, operating under a preschool belief that whoever this was couldn't see me if I couldn't see them. I knew it was stupid, but I didn't care. I didn't want to look!

I could just *feel* that this person was up to no good. Add to that the fact that the footsteps sounded eerily similar to the footsteps I'd heard in the bathroom right before I'd had my head smashed in, and you had a recipe for nearly making me pee my pants.

Okay, so I *did* pee my pants. Just a little. What?! Like you've never done it.

I'm pretty sure my eyes would have stayed closed until scary-foot person did their business in the office and vacated if Trish hadn't started jabbing me in the throat with her elbow. (Once more, don't ask. We were like conjoined twins sharing a very cramped uterus.)

Finally, when it became clear Trish wasn't going to let up until I gagged or opened my eyes, I cracked my lids just in time to see none other than Gavin the sex god sneaking out of Principal's Samedi's private office with a big fat file folder filled with yellowed paper! On his way out, he walked close enough to have reached out and touched us, but he didn't. Instead, he held his thieved file at the perfect angle for me to read the title:

RARE AND FORBIDDEN SPELLS

Not just rare, not just forbidden, but rare *and* forbidden. *That* was what little Mr. Swim Team, Most Likely to

Succeed, I'm-everybody's-friend-and-get-good-grades-and-would-never-rip-out-brains McDougal was lifting from the principal's office.

My eyes bulged, and I jabbed Trish somewhere in the vicinity of her ribcage. I had been so right all along! Gavin was the one to blame. He had the motive, he had opportunity, and now he had stolen a big fat spell folder so he could finish the job he'd started when he'd hacked out those poor, innocent girls' brains.

Trish and I waited until his footsteps faded down the hall before spilling out onto the floor in a grunting pile of bruised internal organs.

"I knew it! We have to go tell Principal Samedi," I said, scrambling to my feet.

"No, we don't! What are we going to say? 'Hey, we were snooping through your office when we saw Gavin McDougal stealing files'? We can't let anyone know we were here. We'll have to find another way to—"

"We don't have time to find another way! He could be boiling Penelope and Kendra's brains in a huge vat of oil right now!"

"I've never heard of any spell that involved boiling brains in oil."

"You're the one who said the spell involved a bunch of brains in a pot."

"But I never said anything about oil. Or boiling," Trish said as we tiptoed toward the door. "Besides, if he's really the one taking brains and—"

"What do you mean 'if'? How much more evidence do you need?" Trish was so mentally challenged when it came to seeing the truth about Gavin. If I didn't know better, I'd think she was crushing even harder than I was—but that was impossible since I *still* wanted to trap Gavin in the janitor's closet and kiss him until our lips turned inside out, no matter how evil he was. I was weak and had totally fallen prey to his sex-god vibe.

"More than we've got now," Trish replied. "So, like I said, *if* he's the one doing this and he really wants to work the super-zombie spell, he's going to need more than two brains. We've got some time."

"Not much," I whispered, a chill running across my skin as we dashed down the hallway back toward the girls' dorm.

Call me crazy, but it didn't feel like we were alone anymore and I could have sworn there was a weird odor drifting from somewhere near the bathrooms. Could have just been generic bathroom stank. Or it could have been the rancid breath of my murderous roomie, or even the pungent aroma of the vinegar Gavin was using to preserve his thieved brains until the time was ripe for his spell to be cast.

Whatever it was, I wasn't ready to go bursting into the bathroom and find out. I'd had my share of nearly getting killed in lavs for the day. I wanted to solve this mystery and get those girls back their brains, but I really didn't want to lose my own in the process.

"So what's our next step? How are we going to prove that Gavin is the harvester before he strikes again?"

"I still think it's Darby and Clarice," Trish said. "Or maybe Principal Samedi trying to make it look like Darby and Clarice."

"Okay, fine." She was going to be proven wrong, but there was no point in wasting time arguing. Right now neither of us had the goods to back up our beliefs. "How are we going to find out for sure? We'll need proof before we start accusing anyone."

Trish turned into the stairwell leading up to our floor, wisely avoiding the elevator, where we might run into more guards or upperclassmen or Resident Assistants. "Let me think about it tonight. I'll stick a note in your locker before class tomorrow and we can go from there."

"Just don't ask me to come meet you in the girls' bathroom." I followed her up the stairs and hovered behind her as she opened the second-floor door.

"I won't." She peeked out into the hall. "All clear. See you in the morning."

"Be careful," I said, feeling strangely anxious about Trish going one way down our hall and I the other. It would be so much better if we could stick together.

"I'll be fine. I'm not the one with the potentially lethal roommate," she said with a grin.

"Thanks."

"Try to sleep with one eye open."

"Right." I rolled my eyes and waved goodbye before

dashing back down the hall and slipping quietly into my room.

My *lonely* room.

Clarice, who had been snoring away when I'd left, was no longer in her bed, which meant she could have been the source of the stank lurking downstairs. For all I knew, she and Darby and Gavin were all three working together. Crap! Trish and I hadn't even thought of that.

Who knew what else we hadn't thought of? Probably lots of things. I just hoped, as I miraculously drifted off to sleep without much trouble at all, that none of those things would end up getting us brain harvested. Or worse.

NINE

Clarice sucks butt.
Karen Vera sucks bigger, dirtier butt.

—*Bathroom stall, second floor girls' bathroom*

I'd been the walking dead for days but hadn't even known it.

I mean, I knew I was a *zombie*, but the social suicide thing was a complete surprise until I entered the cafeteria for lunch on Thursday. I'd been so busy befriending Trish, crushing on Gavin, launching my investigation, being attacked, and dealing with creepy roommates that I'd had no idea just how *horribly* unpopular I was on the way to being—until I saw the writing on the bathroom wall. (Really, I think I ranked somewhere between a used length of dental floss and toe jam. Way below the discarded candied brain bites presently sitting on top of the garbage.)

Trish hadn't been kidding about that whole Deprogrammed-and-Death-Challenged-not-hanging-together thing. It seemed no one knew quite what to do with me, and the nasty looks and narrowed eyes came from both sides of the cafeteria. The Deprogrammed were just as unwilling to clear a chair for me as the DCs were.

My and Trish's cozy two-seater table was occupied by

a pair of sophomores studying for midterms, and Trish herself nowhere to be found. I was forced to circle the lunchroom solo, clutching my tray and feeling my heart rise progressively higher in my throat as back after back turned against me, making it clear I was about as welcome as flesh-eating bacteria.

I, Karen Vera, the girl voted "Most Popular" every year of junior high, was now a lunchroom pariah. I had just about decided to dump my tray and run for the safety of my room when someone called my name.

"Hey, Karen. Over here. We've got a chair free."

I never thought I'd be so relieved to hear the voice of a murderer, but hey, at least he was friendly. Gavin was seated at a table of fit-and-trim swim team guys too intent on feeding their faces to spare me a second glance as I set my tray down and sank gratefully into the chair beside Gavin.

"Thanks," I mumbled. "I was starting to wonder if I had cooties or something."

"Nope, no cooties. At least none that I can see." He smiled and shoved a huge bite of stew from the hot line into his mouth. "But then you can hide a lot under these uniforms."

"True." What was that supposed to mean? I would have smelled an insult, but the smile was throwing me off.

Still trembling slightly from my brush with social death, I picked up my fork but couldn't seem to recover my appetite. I just didn't understand why this was happening. Why was I being lumped into the butt-sucking category with Clarice? I hadn't been mean to anyone, and I'd gone out of my way to smile and remember the names of all the people in my classes. In any case, I'd been here less than a week, so how could I have made so many enemies?

"Hey, you okay?" Gavin asked, though I couldn't help but notice that even his voice wasn't as nice as it had been a couple of days before.

"Yeah, I ... um ... " Okay, this wasn't doing me or the investigation any good. Here I was, cozy with one of my suspects. It would be stupid not to try to get him talking about something, and this situation was really bothering me. "No, I'm not. I don't understand what's going on here. Is everyone always this unfriendly?"

Gavin stared at me for a second, his weirdly electric blue eyes surveying me with suspicion. "No, they're not. But then, it's been a bad week, and most people don't become instant best friends with the shadiest girl at school their first day on campus."

"Clarice is not my friend! She's just my roommate and I'm going to apply for a—"

"I'm not talking about Clarice."

Oh. He wasn't? "You're not?"

"I'm talking about Trish. You didn't really give people a chance to know you as anything but her little sidekick, so—"

"Hold the phone," I said, letting my fork clatter to my tray. "I am *no one's* sidekick." Did that really need to be said? Did I *look* like sidekick material to him?

"Whatever you say." He shrugged in a way that made it clear his sidekick opinion had not been altered in the slightest. Argh!

"Trish has been really nice to me," I said, struggling to keep my cool. "I didn't see any reason not to be her friend. I know all about her being in juvie when she was younger and there were extenuating circumstances that I can completely sympathize with. So if that's the only reason all these people think they're better than she is, then I—"

"No one thinks they're better than she is," Gavin said, loud enough to earn a glance or two from the boys around us before they returned to their meals. (Thank. God. I mean, I'm a fairly confident person, but I didn't know if I could handle the scrutiny of an entire tableful of cute guys.) "*She's* the one with a problem. She's had an attitude about being Deprogrammed from the day she came here."

"So what? That seems valid. The Deprogrammed are obviously not treated fairly."

"Oh, please." He rolled his eyes. "Just because we have to do work-study? Cry me a river."

"Well, that's not really fair, is it?" I asked, feeling sort of stupid but determined not to show it. "That Deprogrammed have to do work-study, but Death Challenged kids don't?"

"The Death Challenged alumni who make the donations that run the school took a vote and decided they didn't want their money to go toward Deprogrammed tuition," Gavin said in between bites of stew. "They thought it would make it harder for the DCs to receive the quality of education they got when they were in school here."

"But that stinks!"

"It's *their* money, and it could have been a lot worse. The alumni could have put pressure on the school board and voted us out of the school altogether." He laid his fork down and turned his full attention to me, making it clear his next point was an important one. "Then Principal Samedi would have had to deactivate every single rogue zombie she'd ever Deprogrammed. You get what that means, right?"

I nodded. "Deactivated" didn't leave a lot of room for interpretation. If the school board hadn't let the Deprogrammed stay, they would have all had to go back to their graves and stay there. The thought of Trish and Gavin six feet under made my bones ache. I couldn't imagine the school without them.

"So work-study seems like a pretty good deal to me," Gavin said, returning to his meal. "Besides, the DCs have to do four years of mandatory public service to the Undead community after they graduate, and Deprogrammed kids don't."

"Oh yeah?" They did? This was news to me. Though I did sort of remember Principal Samedi saying something, during her visit to our house, about being tied up until I was twenty-two. I'd been too busy munching fried brains to pay too much attention, but the community service thing would make sense in that context.

"That's how you reimburse the community for paying for your education. It's also like an apprentice program. You'll learn all about the different jobs available to adult DCs and have a chance to try some of them out. After the four years are done, you can either apply for an Undead job—"

"Like what?" I asked.

"Well, you can work for the High Council as part of the Undead militia or on a Special Ops investigation team," he said, a gleam in his eye that made it clear Gavin found the idea of Special Ops pretty cool. "Or you can teach at one of the schools, do administrative work at the halfway houses for new adult DCs, be a Patroller who checks in to make sure everyone living in the human world is keeping our world top secret—all kinds of stuff."

"And if we don't want to do any of that stuff?" I asked, though the Special Ops thing sounded pretty cool to me too.

"Then you can apply for a visa and go to a human college or get a regular job in the human world. That's what most Deprogrammed people do, work in the regular world like we would have if we hadn't died. It all works out in the end, and no one really stresses out about it."

"But...it doesn't seem that way. It seems like there's major tension around here."

"That's only because of what happened to Kendra and Penelope and the rumors about the spell. And I'm sure Trish isn't helping things with her—" Gavin's mouth snapped closed, and he turned his attention back to his stew. "You know what? Never mind."

"No, tell me what you were going to say. You're sure Trish isn't helping things with what?"

I was starting to get a bad feeling in my stomach about my new BFF. Had she really been exaggerating the stress between the two groups, or was Gavin oblivious because he was a golden boy and immune to the suffering of the masses? And what was this about Trish being shady? That still hadn't been explained to my liking, especially since *Gavin* was the shady character who'd stolen forbidden spells from the principal's office.

"Nothing. None of my business. Besides, you can't be too careful." He shot me another suspicious look, which nearly made me lose it and confront him with his crimes. But I couldn't, not yet.

The worst thing I could do was let him know I was on to him and give him time to cover his tracks. Or worse, make sure I never had the chance to tell anyone what I knew. Looking at Gavin now, with his friendly, open expression and drool-worthy lips, it was hard to believe he'd be capable of taking anyone out, but isn't that what people always say about psycho serial killer types? That they were "so nice and normal" and "the last one you'd suspect of something so heinous"? Meanwhile, the freaks were collecting people's internal organs and storing them in alphabetized freezer bags in their veggie crisper.

Yep, I'd have to tread carefully with Gavin, especially

considering my inherent vulnerability to his particular level of adorableness.

"Trish has done nothing to make me doubt her," I said, forcing myself to take a stab at my meal. "Until I hear some real reason why I shouldn't trust her, something other than a difference of opinion about the state of DC vs. DP politics, I'm going to keep being her friend."

Gavin's mouth quirked up on one side. "Politics?"

"Seems pretty political to me. There are two groups of people being treated differently for reasons having more to do with what they are than who they are or anything they've done."

He rolled his eyes. "You're not going to make the 'this is so like racism' argument, are you? Because there's no way the situation here is anything close to—"

"No, I wasn't going to do that," I said. "But it isn't fair, either. You say it all evens out in the end, but it still stinks that neither side has a choice. What if I'd rather do work-study than waste four years of my life after graduation volunteering? Why shouldn't I have that option, or vice versa?"

"That's just the way it's always been." He shrugged, but looked a little less sure of himself.

"Well, that sounds a lot like what people said when they didn't want women or minorities to have the same rights as everyone else." I shifted uncomfortably in my chair, feeling weirdly like it was my mom's voice coming out of my mouth. I'd always thought she took the feminist thing to an annoying place, but now … I was sort of glad I'd been forced to endure her ranting. "I'm not saying the situation here is the same, but there are similarities."

Gavin chewed thoughtfully for a few seconds. "You might be a little bit right. At least you make a logical argument."

"Thanks." I tried not to grin, but failed. Geez! I was a pathetic flower way too eager to blossom in the rays of Gavin's sun. His sun was evil! And I didn't have petals! I should get up and walk away from him right now before I fell any deeper under his boy-spell.

"You're pretty smart," he said, destroying all hope of resistance. "A lot smarter than you come off at first. What with the big pink bows and all."

"A love for pink bows and intelligence are not mutually exclusive, last time I checked."

"I totally agree," Gavin said. "In fact, I think it would be stupid to underestimate someone just because they happened to be a cute little blond."

Before my heart could quite recover from the explosive bliss of being called a cute little blond, Gavin was gathering his tray and sliding his chair back from the table. Argh! He couldn't leave now! Now, when we'd just started to get somewhere. What did he mean by that last statement? And just *how* cute did he think I was? Like puppy cute or Kate Bosworth in *Blue Crush* cute?

"Yeah, that would be stupid," I agreed, scrambling to think of something to say to keep him at the table. "And superficial."

"Exactly. You can't tell what a person is capable of by looking at their outsides." This sent a little shiver across my skin. What a person was *capable* of? Was he confessing to murder, or had my brain simply begun to degenerate from hunger and prolonged exposure to Gavin's yummy boy-ness? "See you around."

And then he was gone. Leaving me with more questions than I'd had before. Either he'd been taunting me with his last remarks—insinuating that *he* shouldn't be trusted just because he was a hottie—or he was accusing Trish of something, or he actually thought *I* had something to do with all this. I was betting on the first scenario.

If he'd really had something on Trish, wouldn't he have dished when I issued my challenge about needing more than a difference of opinion to doubt my new friend? And how could he *really* think I had anything to do with the brain harvesting? If I'd been the one bashing heads in, I couldn't very well have had my own head bashed, could I? I mean, there was no way I could have given myself a dent the size of the one I was sporting yesterday even if I'd wanted to.

No, it was more likely that Gavin was toying with me. He knew I was on to him and was enjoying playing with my mind for a bit before he got down to the killing-me-to-protect-his-evil-secret part of all this.

"No way. Not going to happen," I muttered aloud, drawing a couple of raised eyebrows from the swim-team boys. But who cared if they thought I was crazy? I'd prove to everyone just who was nuts around here when I caught Gavin red-handed and turned him over to Principal Samedi.

Which might happen even sooner than I'd hoped. I watched Gavin return his tray, but not before he slid something long and silver in his pocket. All the rooms had been checked for illegal weapons after the first murder, so he probably needed to steal an implement of destruction if he planned to keep harvesting. A cafeteria knife wouldn't be the best choice, but if you were desperate enough and strong enough, I guess it could work.

Gavin definitely had the muscles to separate a brain from a head with a butter knife. Now all he needed was the opportunity. From the guilty look on his face as he snuck out the staff exit, he wasn't going to waste any time hunting down that opportunity and another innocent victim!

Moving fast, I ditched my tray of mostly uneaten food at the tray return window and, after waiting a moment or two, scurried out the door where Gavin had just disappeared. I wanted to stay close, but not too close. If he saw me, he'd abort his mission and I'd be forced to endure another twenty-four hours of being the freak, suck-butt girl who'd chosen the wrong best friend. The only chance for me and Trish, or for the girls whose brains had been stolen, was for me to prove Gavin guilty ASAP.

Immediately, if possible. Then everyone would see that Trish and I were heroic, mystery-solving, cool people and not some sort of mucous-like substance best wiped away with a tissue and thrown into the trash.

Luckily, I caught sight of Gavin at the end of the long gray hall just as he turned left, but he didn't see me. I scurried after him, my black ballet flats barely making a sound as I ran. Thank goodness I'd gone for comfort over height-enhancement this morning. Anything with heels would have been making way too much noise.

As it was, I was able to trail my prey with the soft tread of a jungle cat, silently weaving through the maze of hallways until the scent of chlorine filled the air. Crap. Was Gavin just sneaking off for some extra swim practice? If so, I was going to feel like a complete dink, but there was no way I could turn back now. Deep in my bones, I was certain the boy ahead of me was up to no good.

Besides … if seeing my crush splashing around in his regulation Speedo was the worst thing to happen to me today, I wouldn't complain. I mean, it wasn't like I was a professional boy-ogler or anything, but if the opportunity presented itself…

Doing my best not to be distracted by visions of cute boys in spandex, I watched Gavin disappear through a heavy blue door. Silently, I counted to ten before easing the door open, peeking inside … and screaming my head off.

I couldn't help it. All stealth abandoned me in the instant I saw the pool.

I just wasn't prepared. I mean, I'd hoped to get some dirt on Gavin and maybe even catch him in the act of trying to harvest a brain, but there was no way I expected his next victim to already be dead, floating in a cloud of red in the center of the DEAD High pool.

TEN

No eating, drinking, or running on the pool deck.
No swimming within one hour of eating or within
twenty-four hours of receiving a serious flesh
wound. Undead flesh WILL begin to disintegrate
if chlorine is introduced into an open sore.

—*Pool Rules, DEAD High*

I was drawn to the edge of the pool like a shop-a-holic to
a fifty-percent-off sale. Gavin was nowhere to be seen, so
there was nothing to keep my feet from wandering closer
and closer to the body, or to keep my stupid eyes from
staring at the limp figure in the pool until my brain eventually connected the dots. Even with the side of her head
cracked open, it didn't take long to realize who that signature brown bob belonged too.

Then there were the ballet flats. We'd joked about wearing the exact same shoes only a couple of hours ago, just
after first period when Trish had told me she was going to
investigate a lead. She hadn't had time to tell me what the
lead was or why she didn't want me along for the investigating, however, which had annoyed the heck out of me.

What was with the solo act all of a sudden? Weren't we
a team?

I'd made her promise to tell all at lunch, but she hadn't shown up. Because she'd been getting herself *killed*, and I'd been too busy stressing about my popularity or lack thereof and chatting with Gavin to actually go looking for my friend. And now, she was dead. Dead!

This *couldn't* be happening!

"Ohmygod, ohmygod, ohmygod." I didn't know how long I'd been chanting the same phrase over and over again, but eventually I realized I was responsible for the shrill soundtrack to this horrific moment and that I should probably shut up while I still had the chance.

I slapped my hand over my mouth, muffling my hysterical episode as I shuffled away from the edge of the pool, toward the door. Trish was dead! Trish. *My* Trish was floating there with her brain swiped from her poor, innocent skull.

Deep breath. I was almost to the door. I had to get out of here, had to get help before—

A second later, a larger, manlier hand covered mine and I was pulled backward into about five-feet-eight inches of swimmer-muscled flesh. "Shh! Keep quiet, and do exactly as I say."

It was Gavin! He'd snuck up behind me and was going to gouge open my head with his appropriated kitchen knife and add my brain to his unholy collection. My life, and Trish's, hung in the balance!

If I couldn't get free and report him, forcing him to reveal the location of the brains he'd stolen, all would be lost. Principal Samedi would never suspect her star athlete and pet pupil of this kind of thing. He'd be the last person on her list. By the time she figured out Gavin was responsible—*if* she figured it out at all—it would be too late to reunite the victims with their brains.

I had to fight him.

And when your captor has seven inches and a few dozen pounds on you, the only way to fight is dirty.

"Ow!!" Gavin hissed in pain as I dug my nails into his hand and delivered a wicked stomp to the arch of his foot. But he didn't let go. Instead, his arms tightened around me as he captured my wrists in his other large, manly hand. Argh! A boy who died at sixteen shouldn't have hands this large! He was clearly a freak of nature who used his abnormally big hands not only for paddling through the water with great speed but for killing innocent girls.

Why not harvest the brains of other guys? Why not give himself a challenge instead of picking on people who were naturally smaller and weaker than he was? He wasn't just a murdering psycho, he was a bully, and for some reason that made me even madder.

Using every last bit of my strength, I rammed my foot back into his shin bone. Unfortunately, all I received for my efforts was to be squeezed so tightly I couldn't breathe.

"Karen, stop it. I'm not going to hurt you."

Likely story. That's probably what he said to all the girls whose brains he harvested. "Oh, I'm not going to hurt you, just come over here and look at my large, manly hands," and then—wham! He struck. Like a python or a scorpion or an alien with acid for blood who'd been hiding in the ceiling waiting for a meal while the entire crew of the spaceship turned on each other and made the alien's job even easier by fighting when they should have been bonding together for the common good.

Or something like that.

I thrashed as Gavin picked me up and began hauling me the last few feet toward the door. I kicked and struggled, making this abduction as difficult as possible, but finally had to give it up when the world started to spin. Geez...I was getting dizzy; I really needed to breathe. Wonder why that was?

Zombies don't have a pulse so I knew my heart wasn't working anymore, but my lungs obviously were. Still, an Undead person couldn't be killed by suffocation—we'd learned in Health that the only thing that could take us down was decapitation or severe trauma to the brain. So I wondered what would happen to me if I did pass out from lack of oxygen. Would I just stay unconscious until I was allowed to breathe again? Or at least until Gavin managed to pry my brain from my skull and throw me into the pool along with Trish?

The mental image conjured by that thought helped me summon the strength for one last round of thrashing. Gavin's hold slipped...I squirmed...and score! I had freedom! I darted to the right, booking it toward the bleachers that lined one side of the pool, not thinking anything but that I had to put as much space between Gavin and me as possible. There had to be another exit somewhere. If I could just move fast and—

"No!" My feet tangled in my stupid, oversized black robe and I fell to the ground with a grunt.

"Shh!" Gavin grabbed me under the arms and his hand smashed over my mouth once more. "Karen, come on! I'm not the bad guy. You've got to trust me. And be quiet!" He hauled me deep into the darkness beneath the bleachers, then crouched in the shadows, pulling me down with him until I was sort of sitting on his lap.

I was probably the closest I'd ever been to a boy. The fact that he was also an incredibly cute boy and smelled rather delightfully of pool and French fries and soap was enough to make a tiny thrill of girlish delight penetrate the fog of fear.

Never would I claim hormones help a person think more clearly. But in this case, they made me realize that I might have misjudged my present situation and prompted me to do a quick review of the facts.

First of all, Gavin hadn't killed me. He could have just smashed me over the head while I was distracted by the sight of Trish's watery grave, but he hadn't. Secondly, he kept telling me he wasn't going to hurt me, even after I'd done my best to rough him up. Thirdly, it seemed an awful lot like we were hiding back here under the bleachers, and why would we be hiding if Gavin was the murderer? There would be nothing to hide *from* and certainly no heavy, scary footsteps sounding out on the tiles surrounding the pool.

I froze, every muscle in my body tensing as I strained to hear exactly where the footsteps were coming from and where they were headed. They were definitely on this side of the pool. Oh no. Why hadn't I let Gavin pull me out the door while we had the chance?

As if he sensed the shift in the direction of my stressing, Gavin's hand eased from my mouth and his arms relaxed so I was no longer pinned in place. I turned and shot him my most confused *what the heck is going on, spill all now* look.

But he only shook his head and pressed a finger to his lips. He didn't know who we were hiding from either, but he didn't want to take any chances.

Or he was stalling until his accomplice reached our location.

A second ago that suspicion would have been enough to make me bolt for freedom once more and take my chances on outrunning Gavin and whoever this other person was, but now I stayed where I was. Something in Gavin's eyes told me he was as scared as I was, and just as disturbed by discovering Trish's body floating in the pool. Judging from his behavior the past few minutes, it looked like I'd had the wrong guy.

But if Gavin wasn't responsible, who was? And why had Gavin just happened to be the one to discover Trish? Unlucky coincidence, or something more? And what about the spells he'd lifted from Samedi's office?

I didn't know what to think. All I knew was that the footsteps were getting closer and closer, and I couldn't see a darn thing through the spaces between the seats. The bleachers weren't fully extended so there wasn't even any light coming in from the front, only from the side where we'd crawled in. The other side was flat against the wall.

It felt like we were in a cave, a very creepy cave with a predator lurking somewhere in the shadows nearby. Whether Gavin was the predator or the person outside was, I suddenly decided I didn't want to stick around to find out. I still had time to get out from under the bleachers, across the few feet of pool deck, and reach the door. It couldn't be too late!

And this time, I wouldn't make the mistake of forgetting I was fashionably challenged.

I lifted the bottom of my robe and bolted for the light, only to trip over a piece of metal and go sprawling back to the ground. When had I become so uncoordinated? I was a trained cheer athlete!

The good news was that I was up and running again in a few seconds, despite the tingling in my legs indicating they'd fallen asleep sometime between crouching down and standing up again. The bad news was that Gavin was hot on my heels and the footsteps outside were running too. And it sounded like they were a heck of a lot faster than either me or Gavin.

The metal fixtures supporting the bleachers started screaming just as Gavin grabbed my wrist and pulled. "Get down!"

"No, let go. Let—" My words turned into a cry of pain as the bleacher seats slammed into my right side.

The seats were collapsing. Whoever was out there was shutting the bleachers up the rest of the way, knowing Gavin and I were inside! If they succeeded in closing them completely, we'd both be smashed flatter than the fried-brain-and-potato pancakes the cafeteria had served for breakfast this morning.

Shock at realizing I was about to be crushed and the pressure of Gavin's hand finally convinced me to hit the ground. I landed in the dust accumulated beneath the bleachers just as the seat above my head collapsed. I scooted as fast as I could toward the wall, following Gavin's lead.

We were only buying time, and maybe only a few seconds of it, but the urge to survive was strong enough to make those few seconds seem vital. The world had narrowed to avoiding the crush of the metal closing in on our right for as long as possible, dodging the killing blow until there was no other choice but to take our medicine.

Take your medicine—what a stupid phrase darted through my mind, followed closely by *I wonder if our killer knew we were here all along or if I tipped them off when I fell? I wonder if it's my fault Gavin's about to die?*

Then the metal gave one last mighty screech and slammed into our sides. Gavin took the brunt of the hit, being wider, but the bleachers came for me soon enough. The person outside had shoved hard enough and fast enough that there was no problem with momentum.

I screamed again and I think Gavin did too, but I couldn't be certain. After a second my ears stopped working and then my mouth, as if both had been swallowed whole. The pain came then, but it was mercifully brief, only a flash of white-hot agony and then everything went soft and dark.

All in all, not the worst way to die. Though if I'd had my choice, I would have picked that evening at the football field. At least the sun was setting sweetly in the sky, and I hadn't been forced to see my new BFF floating face down in a pool, or know the guy I'd been crushing on—who'd probably done nothing more than try to save my life—was dying along with me. And it was All. My. Fault.

———

Brains, brains, the magical food. The more you eat them, the more you ... are so supremely grateful that you're a zombie and not a normal girl, because if you were normal you would be totally dead. Even taking brains all smushed up via some sort of tube inserted directly into the stomach—ew, I know, very gross, but actually not as painful as it sounds—wasn't something I was going to complain about.

"Don't touch it and try to lie completely still," Dr. Connor was saying, shaking her head wearily. "I hope you realize how close you and your boyfriend came to something even an infusion wouldn't fix."

Oh my god. She'd just called Gavin my boyfriend. Had

he told her I was his girlfriend? Or had she just assumed we were a couple because we were found under the bleachers together? I was dying to know, but couldn't ask. How immature would that have seemed, to be more concerned about whether some guy had called me his girlfriend than nearly dying?

Whoa. Dying. I had nearly died. Permanently this time, of something a whole lot more serious than a whack on the back of the head. Someone had tried to *murder* me, and Gavin too. Murder. Like, *for real* murder (I go to the *Encarta World Dictionary* to reinforce how serious and real this is):

MURDER:
   n. The crime of killing another person deliberately and not in self-defense or with any other extenuating circumstance recognized by law.
   v. To kill somebody with great violence and brutality, to put an end to or destroy something.

Dr. Connor stared at me in the dim light, as if she realized I needed some time for the full scariness of what had happened to sink in, which it did. Big time.

"Can I call my mom and dad?" I asked, sounding about three years old.

Man, did I want to go home right now. I didn't want to investigate anything. I didn't want to discover who had tried to murder Gavin and me. I didn't want to find out what kind of cute he thought I was or whether or not he returned my crushy feelings. I just wanted out of this crazy place before it was too late—before I ended up like Trish.

Oh no. Poor Trish. I'd nearly forgotten about what had happened to her in all the excitement of regaining consciousness in the infirmary for the second time in two days.

"Shh, just lie still." Dr. Connor smoothed my hair away from my face with her soft, papery-feeling hands. "We'll call your parents as soon as you're up and about. Though I doubt this is the kind of news they're looking forward to on a Friday morning."

"It's Friday? But I thought—"

"You've been out for over twelve hours. You and Gavin both." She shook her head again, as if I'd done this on purpose to hurt her feelings. She was a whiz with the guilt thing. Even better than my mother. "I have seen far too much of you already, Miss Vera. If I don't give you so much as a Band-Aid between now and the day you graduate, I will be a happy woman." She turned away, but I wasn't alone for long.

"You're awake." Principal Samedi did not sound entirely happy about this development.

"Um…yeah." I blinked, trying to get my eyes to adjust. It seemed so dark. I was in the school infirmary, but even without the fluorescent lights, the white walls should have made the room brighter than this.

"Don't strain yourself. Your eyes are still healing. It

will probably be a few more hours before your organs are fully functional. You and Gavin were both very, very badly hurt," Samedi said. As if this was not clear to me, what with the giant tube in my stomach and all. "What in the world were you thinking, crawling around behind half-closed bleachers?"

"We were hiding from whoever harvested Trish's brain and threw her in the pool," I said, beginning to think Samedi hadn't gotten the murder memo. "Then the brain stealer realized we were there and tried to kill us by closing up the bleachers."

Samedi was quiet for several seconds, making me wish I could see her face more clearly. Was she shocked? Or was this old news? Could Samedi really have something to do with the brain harvesting epidemic sweeping the school? Trish had certainly thought so. Was that why she'd become the next victim?

"Gavin will confirm this story?" Samedi finally asked, a hint of suspicion in her tone. Oh no. No way, she *wasn't* going there, not after what I'd been through the past few days.

"He most certainly will. Just ask him." My tone made it clear I wasn't pleased or intimidated ... at least not much. After all, what could she do to me with Dr. Connor across the room?

"Gavin will have the chance to tell his side of the story as soon as he regains consciousness."

"Oh god, is he okay? He's not—"

"He's going to be fine," she said, sounding nicer for a second. "We're expecting him to wake up any moment now."

"Good. He'll tell you the same thing. Someone tried to kill us."

"Did you get a look at this person?"

"No," I admitted. "But we heard footsteps, and they sounded a lot like the heavy footsteps I heard in the bathroom the other day."

Samedi made a grunting sound under her breath. "You do have a gift for being in the wrong place at the wrong time, Karen."

"Trish and I were trying to help catch the person who was shoplifting people's brains." I figured I might as well come clean. If Samedi was the one responsible, she already knew what I'd been up to. If she wasn't, knowing Trish might have been closing in on the identity of the harvester might help her figure out who was responsible. Either way, I had nothing to lose. "She said she was going to investigate a lead and we'd talk about it during lunch, but then she never showed up so I went looking for her."

"And how did you know to look in the pool?" Samedi asked, that same wary note in her tone. She really seemed to think I had been up to something shady, which was just *insane*.

I was about to tell her so, when Gavin piped up from across the room.

"She was with me." I turned my head in his direction,

but couldn't see much. He was just a dark lump lying on a bed against the far wall. "Karen's thinking about joining the girls' team. I was going to show her around."

Lies. Gavin was full of lies, but I didn't say a word to contradict him.

After all, he *had* tried to save my life. So far, all Principal Samedi had done was ask a bunch of questions and refrain from calling my parents the first time I was attacked by a maniac. Between the two of them—even taking into account his spell theft—I had to trust Gavin. At least for the moment.

"We'd just gotten to the pool when we saw Trish, then we heard a noise in the men's locker room. We hid because we thought it might be the harvester coming back." He groaned and I heard Dr. Connor urging him to lie still. "Guess we were right."

"What you were was lucky." Principal Samedi sighed. "I've warned everyone to stay in populated areas, and I certainly made it clear no students were to get involved in the investigation. I'm disappointed, Karen. You've only been here a few days, but you're old enough to understand the importance of rules."

"I'm sorry. I was just trying to help."

"I won't say anything else. I think what happened to your friend is punishment enough for your poor decision making." Ouch. Low blow, Samedi. "But rest assured there will be consequences if your respect for authority doesn't improve. Quickly."

She had spun on her heel and vacated the infirmary before I could think of what to say. Which was probably for the best. Despite a healthy fear of grown-ups-in-positions-of-power in my former life, I wasn't feeling the love (or fear, or respect, or whatever) for my new principal.

Either she was completely incapable and her incompetence was getting her students killed, or she was in on the whole thing. Neither option filled me with warm fuzzies or the urge to obey her word as law. It also didn't inspire much hope for Trish. If I stopped searching for the truth, Trish was as good as dead. I felt that truth deep in my brain-filled belly.

I had to find a way to stay at DEAD and track down the person responsible for terrorizing my new school before it was too late. But first, I had to nap. Turns out nearly getting killed takes a lot out of a girl. And a guy. Gavin was already snoring across the room.

As I drifted off to sleep, I couldn't help but get a tiny thrill out of the fact that I knew Gavin McDougal snored. Maybe that made me a dork. But if that was dorkiness, I didn't want to be cool.

ELEVEN

Library due dates will be strictly enforced. Failure to return borrowed materials in a timely fashion will result in fines and the forfeit of borrowing privileges. Books may be checked out for two weeks, DVDs for one week, and spell books and flesh specimens for up to twenty-four hours.

You must have a note from your teacher to take magical materials or samples of Undead flesh out of the library. If acid, flesh-eating bacteria or maggots are required for your experiment, you will need to check out those materials from your science teacher and keep all potentially dangerous materials in the school lab.

Do not bring food into the library! We are not an alternative to the cafeteria!

—*Library Policies, DEAD High*

Meet me in the library during lunch. Come alone! G.

—*Note found on Karen Vera's locker*

———————

G, hmmmm…

Despite the oddly girly, curlycue quality of the script, I was guessing the note was from Gavin. It had to be. I didn't know anyone else at DEAD with a *G* name.

(They're fairly rare. Try to think of another one. I'll wait…Rare, right? Especially for girls. I mean, you've got Gareth or Garth—gag—for boys, but Giselle is the only girl *G* name I can think of. Or Gertie. But who would name their child Gertie in the twenty-first century? A sadist, or a criminal, or someone with a really tragic sense of humor, that's who.)

I shoved the note in my pocket and furtively checked the space on both sides of my locker. I was alone. Thank. God. The last thing I needed was to be observed reading illicit communications from my partner in crime. Or partner in *solving* crime, as Gavin would obviously have it. I'd already spent my early morning hours—six a.m. is not a good time to be awake even if you're not getting yelled at—in the office with my parents and Principal Samedi. Samedi had changed her recent let's-keep-this-between-us tune and called my parents at the buttcrack of dawn to tell them that I was in the infirmary.

Once my parents learned I was hurt, they bundled the trips into their car seats and came right away. It was so great to see their faces—all five of them—when I woke up for the second time. Even if Mom and Dad were furious about me snooping around, putting myself in danger, I was still glad I had the chance to get in a few hugs before they'd headed for home and I'd headed to class.

At the moment things were fairly cool, but if Samedi even smelled the ink of a subversive note on my finger-tips, I'd be toast. She wasn't happy with me. Not happy at all. My eyes had been in perfect working order by the time of our meeting, and I hadn't missed the scowl-glares coming from her direction. There was no doubt how very displeased she was with her newest student.

My parents, on the other hand, though obviously concerned, seemed weirdly resigned to me being stuck at the high school of death. Once they heard I might have been targeted by a psycho who would think nothing of tracking me down at my family's home, they'd backtracked on their intention to cart me home first and ask questions later. With the three babies, they just couldn't risk a homicidal maniac attack the way they could have before the trips were born.

I mean, we could have sought refuge at a hotel or with obscure relatives or something, but my parents didn't think of that and I wasn't about to help them out. As much as it stung to realize that my life and safety didn't seem as important to them as the lives of their smaller, cuter, droolier kids, I couldn't give in to the urge to beg Mommy and Daddy to protect me. Trish and two other girls were counting on me. And maybe counting on Gavin, too.

But *he* still had some major explaining to do. No way was I letting him off the hook for his theft from Samedi's office. He was going to have to do some fast talking before I agreed to whatever scheme he had planned. Guess the library was as good a place for him to do his explaining as any.

I grabbed a dried brain bar (dehydrated brains with a little oat thrown in, surprisingly tasty as well as portable) from the vending machine and slipped into the library, easily finding Gavin seated at a sunny table in the corner.

Sigh. Who was I kidding? I would probably agree to dress like a homeless clown and perform the chicken dance on the popular kids' lunch table if Gavin asked me to. The power of his tractor-beam eyes had increased at least tenfold since I'd last seen him. The look he shot me was so intense, in fact, that I actually forgot how to breathe and walk at the same time, and I ended up stumbling the last few feet to the table.

Geez. When did he get so cute? I mean, he'd always been gorgeous, but today he was ... a young zombie god. Surely girls everywhere fell to their knees to worship him as he strolled through the halls.

"Hey," he said, nodding at me though his gaze moved to survey the rest of the library, on the lookout for spies. We were both completely paranoid. It had to be true love. It just had to be.

"Hey." I sat down, talking my muscles through each movement and praying I would recover normal motor function soon. This level of girlie reaction was not healthy or conducive to catching a killer.

"You look ... different," Gavin said, still not meeting my eyes.

"Oh? Um ... must be the whole getting-crushed thing. Maybe I'm not completely back to normal yet." I tore open my brain bar, completely mortified. I *knew* I should have eaten breakfast, no matter what Dr. Connor had said about giving my stomach some time to heal after she removed my tube.

Of course, a little quality time with my makeup bag would have been a good idea too. Why had I forgone primping in the name of being on time to first period? Mr. Cork was scary, but apparently so was my face.

"No, it's not that," Gavin said. "You look..." Electric blue eyes met mine, and I'm pretty sure I had an out-of-body experience. At least I couldn't feel my fingers or toes for a few seconds. "You look really good. That feeding tube thing agreed with you."

Oh. My. God. Was it possible? Was it possible that I had been transformed into a young zombie goddess, similar to Gavin's transformation into a young zombie god? My nonbeating heart was so excited, I swear I thought I felt it pump a few times, defying logic and zombie physiology in the name of Gavin McDougal.

If I'd been alone, I would have totally ripped open my notebook and begun a page of *Karen Anne McDougals*, but instead I played it cool, giving my not-so-recently washed hair a little flip over my shoulder and shooting Gavin a smile. "Thanks. I feel good, though I still can't believe we almost died."

"Yeah, thanks to you," he said, the sudden scowl on his face putting an abrupt end to my imaginings of what our children would look like (if we weren't both dead and therefore unable to reproduce). "Why were you following me?"

"Because I thought you were the harvester," I said. Little Mr. Perfect thought he was above suspicion, but I had his number. "Now, why don't *you* tell *me* why you were stealing spells from Samedi's office?"

"What?" He laughed, an innocent laugh I would have bought if I didn't know better. "I don't know what—"

"I was there, snooping with Trish, so don't try to deny it. I saw you."

"Snooping? For what? Why don't you tell me—"

"No, I asked first. So tell me what you were up to, and why you were really headed to the pool, because we both know I'm not joining the girls' swim team."

"Why not?" he asked, covering his surprise at having his theft discovered rather well. "You got something against athletics?"

"No, I've got something against green hair. Naturally blond hair and chlorine—they just don't mix."

"So you're saying your hair color is natural?" His perfectly shaped (bushy but not too bushy) eyebrows arched in mock surprise.

Oh. My. God. He didn't go there. How could I have been thinking this dude was a god a few seconds ago? He was clearly in league with the forces of evil.

"Is there any doubt?" I struggled to keep my cool. "I mean, look at my freaking roots. Do you see any darkness there?"

"Hey, I'm a guy. What do I know about that stuff?" He shrugged. "But I've heard the phrase 'bleached blond' tossed around a few times when mentioning a certain new girl with poor taste in friends."

"I've heard the phrase 'conceited jerk' tossed around a few times when mentioning a certain swim-team dork," I said, though I'd actually heard nothing of the sort. "Quit trying to avoid my questions. And don't you dare talk about Trish that way." That made Gavin wince, and I knew I had him. He felt lousy for that last crack. Now it was time to go in for the kill. "Why were you taking those spells?"

"I…I thought I could figure out who had attacked Penelope and Kendra."

"By working a spell?" I prompted, amazed at my own detective-like interrogation techniques. Maybe I was the one with a future in law enforcement. "A rare and forbidden spell? Doesn't that seem pretty risky?"

"I've been studying magic since I came here." Gavin got all scowly again. "I know what I'm doing, probably better than just about anyone at school."

"Even better than Darby or my creepy roommate?"

"They're beginners," he said, clearly not impressed. "Worse than beginners—they're dabblers. I doubt either one of them has ever followed the proper protocol. That's why none of their stupid spells work."

"But yours do?"

"Yeah. They do." I swear he stuck his nose up in the air a little bit. He was soooo cocky. It actually reminded me of someone, though I couldn't quite put my finger on who. "That's how I knew to go to the pool. The spell I'd cast the night before indicated the harvester would strike near water. And it's not like there's a lot of water on campus besides the pool."

"Then why didn't you go there earlier? Or warn everyone to stay away?" I was getting a little sniffly as my mind flashed on the image of Trish floating face-down in a cloud of her own blood. "If you had, Trish might still have her brain."

Gavin's eyes shifted and he suddenly became very busy digging around in his backpack for a pencil and paper. "I wasn't sure if I was right. I'd never done that spell before and—"

"And you were afraid of being wrong. Trish is dead because you didn't want to look like a doofus."

"That's not true. I couldn't very well tell everyone I'd been casting illegal spells. Samedi's head would explode. She does her best to get rid of anyone who tries to learn about normal magic, let alone—"

"Yeah. That's what Trish said. That's why Trish thought she was responsible for the harvesting." I briefly filled Gavin in on the theory that Samedi was trying to get rid of Darby and Clarice. "But I've been thinking about it, and I really don't think Samedi has anything to do with this, even if she did taste my blood the other day while I was unconscious."

"Taste your blood?" he asked, not sounding as grossed out as I'd thought he would.

"Yeah. Trish said she saw Samedi take a little … taste."

Blerchk. My brain bar was no longer tasting nearly as yummy.

"Wow." He shook his head and started writing something in his notepad. "She totally thinks you're guilty too. Or at least she did."

"What?!"

"She was checking to see if you'd been eating other zombies. If you'd been chowing on anything but animal brains, your blood would have tasted funny and Samedi would have known you were the one responsible."

"Me? But I—"

"Look totally guilty. I mean, didn't the harvesting start the *day* after you came here? And there's the issue of who you were hanging with. I bet Samedi thought the two of you were working together. I had the same thought myself, though I mostly thought Trish was working alone. I didn't think you were smart enough. At least not at first."

"Okay, spill it," I said, refusing to get distracted by the bashing of my intelligence. "What do you have on Trish? You keep saying she's shady and suspicious but—"

"She *is* shady and suspicious."

"Why?" I asked, frustration making my voice louder than it should have been.

"Shh!" Gavin glared first at me, then at the rest of the room, only continuing when he was sure my outburst hadn't attracted attention. "Her first roommate died last year under very sketchy circumstances. I'm guessing she didn't share that with her new BFF."

Oh. God. No, she hadn't. But that didn't mean anything, right? Maybe she'd just been waiting for the right time … like there was ever a right time to tell someone a lot of people thought you were a roommate killer.

Gavin continued with a smug look on his face. "Nobody could ever prove Trish had anything to do with it, and Principal Samedi and the investigators from the High Council said it was just an accidental case of milk overdose, but no one would room with her after that. That's why she has a single even though she's only a freshman."

Trish hadn't said anything about being investigated either, but I could totally understand that. No one wants to brag about being on the wrong side of the interrogation desk. "Milk overdose? You can really die from that?"

"It's the lactic acid. It does something to the soft tissue of some zombies, makes it degenerate really fast or something," he said, making the word "degenerate" sound way sexier than I'd imagined possible. But then, he could probably give a speech about mealworms and transfix the female population. "They thought Trish's roommate had been injected with a concentrated dose, but couldn't find a needle hole."

I nibbled my bottom lip, letting Gavin's story digest. "So … she was innocent as far as anyone knows?"

"Well, yeah, but—"

"So, there you go. She was probably innocent then, and we *know* she's innocent now."

Gavin looked guilty again. "Yeah. She wasn't my favorite person, but seeing her like that…"

We both fell silent, giving Trish the moment of respect she deserved.

"She said she was following a lead, but she didn't tell me what it was." I leaned closer, suddenly worried someone might overhear our conversation. That weird "watched" feeling from a few nights ago had returned with a vengeance. And it might have been my imagination, but I thought I caught of whiff of stank as well.

I didn't dare start sniffing too obviously, however, for fear Gavin would think I had some sort of chronic sinus condition. I'd once refused to dance with a boy in sixth grade because of sinus issues and knew what a serious turn-off repetitive sniffing could be. Almost as bad as smacking your food or slurping the milk from your cereal out of the side of the bowl.

"You can't even guess what she was looking into?" he asked, pulling my mind away from my list of *Most Annoying Human Habits*. "You two were snooping around the office, right? Did you find anything?"

I filled Gavin in on the tardy records revealing that both Darby and Clarice were late to class the day Penelope lost her brains. "I'm thinking Trish had something on Darby and Clarice. Or at least Clarice. Something more than what we found in the office. Clarice wasn't in our room when I got back after midnight, and I bet—"

"But Clarice is so... I don't know, she seems like she's all talk," Gavin said, though I saw him print Clarice's name on his paper. "Do you really think she'd have it in her? To gouge out three other girls' brains?"

"I don't know, but she was certainly hacked off at Trish the other night. She threatened her, right in front of me, and she's been acting really weird."

"Weird how?"

"She spends an awful lot of time hiding out under a black blanket, grunting at her chicken bones. And she'll start crying for, like, no reason at all, and she seems to have some sort of allergy to the color pink. I think my Hello Kitty pajamas made her break out in hives."

Gavin smiled. "That sounds pretty normal for Clarice. She's just … not all there."

"The girl voted *Least Likely for Anyone to Want to Room With* two years in a row?"

"Except for Trish, yeah. But at least Clarice never killed anyone."

"That we know of. She might have decided to start," I said. "And I'd really appreciate it if you'd stop acting like Trish is a criminal. I never got any creep vibes from her, and I'm usually good at picking up on things like that."

"Creep vibes, huh? Like the ones you got from me?" he asked, a hint of hurt in his expression. "You thought I was guilty, right?"

"No, not really," I confessed, my nonbeating heart doing that weird squeezing thing again as I met his eyes. "I mean, the evidence was pointing your way, but in my gut I was pretty sure you were innocent. Otherwise I would have never been able to … "

Ohmygod! What was up with the verbal spew? I'd nearly confessed my undying crush-i-tude right to Gavin's *face*. I clearly needed a lot more sleep and some raw brains and maybe a pedicure. (Pedicures always improve my brain function. I think it has something to do with the stimulation of acupressure points in the foot or something. Or maybe it's the exfoliation factor. Surely shedding dead skin cells had to boost your mind power.)

"Never been able to what?"

"Um...follow you. To the pool. I never would have been able to follow you to the pool. I would have been too afraid."

"You should have been too afraid. If I'd been guilty, I could have totally taken you," he said, getting this big brotherly tone in his voice I didn't entirely care for. "You've got to be careful, Karen. You do realize you're, like, abnormally wee, right?"

Abnormally wee? Abnormally *wee*? Was he *trying* to bring out my murderous side or something? Didn't he realize you just don't say things like that to short people? That we found such size-ist attitudes extremely insulting?

"Don't hit me," he said, holding his hands up in front of his face. "I just meant that anyone on campus could beat you in a fight, and I don't want to see you get hurt. That's why I think we should stick together. It's obvious you're not going to stop until you find out who did this, and—"

"But maybe Clarice couldn't," I said, a mental breakthrough banishing my short-person anger and the thrill of knowing my crush was worried about my delicate self being taken out by a brain harvester. "She's not much bigger than

I am. Maybe an inch or two taller but not big on the muscles. How could she overpower three girls, all of them taller and heavier than she is?"

"You realize you're blowing holes in your own theory."

"I know." I sighed and dropped my head into my hands. "We just need more to go on, and we have to hurry. If we don't find Kendra's brain right away, we'll be too late. Principal Samedi said she only had three or four days, tops."

"We'll find something. Don't worry," he said, though he didn't sound nearly as confident as I would have liked. "And maybe Principal Samedi and her people will figure something out."

I lifted my head. "It doesn't seem like they're trying that hard though, does it?"

"I don't know. Samedi looked pretty tired this morning." Gavin shrugged. "I haven't seen her around the school much the past few days, but she must be doing something to—"

"Wait," I whispered, wrinkling my nose. The stink was definitely somewhere nearby, which meant we weren't alone. "Come on, let's get out of here."

"You smell it? I was wondering if it was just me," Gavin hissed, shoving his pencil and paper back into his bag. "I think I smelled it yesterday too, right after the bleachers collapsed, before I blacked out."

"I know what I just said about Clarice, but she does have some horrendous breath. And I smelled something weird in the hallway after Trish and I broke into Samedi's office," I said, swallowing hard. I tried to play it cool when Gavin grabbed my hand and pulled me between two tall bookshelves.

"What about when you were attacked in the bathroom?" he asked.

I thought for a second, racking my brain for some sort of scent memory, but couldn't remember smelling anything other than standard bathroom-variety odor. "No, I didn't smell it then. Which is weird, don't you—"

Gavin's fingers touched my lips, sending a shiver of electricity across my skin. It was like my lips had never been touched before, as if, prior to contact with the magic McDougal fingers, they were so much lumpy, nerveless dough and only now were experiencing the true magnificence of their lipfulness.

It was enough to make my knees go a little weak, and this was just hand-to-lip contact. If ever his lips should meet mine, I almost feared the consequences. (Though not enough to keep me from praying with every cell in my body that Gavin was pulling me back between the shelves for a pre-investigation make-out session. Kissing had to be better for brain function than pedicures or exfoliation. The locking of our lips was, therefore, practically a *necessity*! Surely Gavin had realized the same.)

Sadly, however, our love was not to be. At least not right then. We had more pressing issues than lip-locking— like catching the killer a few feet away.

TWELVE

The dead walk beneath.
In the shadows long creeping,
secret lives unfold.

—Undead Haiku, author unknown, Zombie Poets
Through the Ages, 2nd Edition

———————

Gavin pointed through the stacks of books. A few rows over, a figure in a black robe stood suspiciously close to the section on black magic. I couldn't see his or her face, but the stink was definitely stronger in this corner of the library. This had to be our would-be killer! I mean, how many people in one school could smell this foul?

My partner in crime-solving must have come to a similar conclusion, because he started inching toward the end of the aisle, trying to get a better look at our suspect. I followed, moving with the same pantherlike grace with which I'd tailed Gavin to the pool. I was getting really good at the lurking and sneaking, if I do say so myself. The only sound was the faint rustle of my robe as I moved.

Unfortunately, the Stenchful One must have had amazing hearing—or a sixth sense that warned about being stalked—because they suddenly bolted.

"Crap! Come on!" Gavin grabbed my hand again and

booked it around our shelf and down the aisle where we'd last seen the figure in black.

We turned the corner in time to see a black door in the wall, decorated with paintings of red-eyed snakes, slam closed as the hem of what looked like a standard-issue school uniform robe swished out of sight. Gavin raced forward, grabbing the handle as if he meant to pursue whoever this was into whatever strange place a creepy door like this led to. But a few tugs revealed that it was locked from the inside.

"I can't believe this." He kicked the door with one non-regulation Converse. "We were so close to getting the freak responsible for all this."

"Not really," I said, hating to burst his bubble but knowing we had to keep ourselves from jumping to conclusions if we really wanted to get to the bottom of our mystery. "Just because this person smelled and the person who shut us up in the bleachers smelled doesn't mean they're the brain harvester. Or even the same person. And this person might have just been ... nervous or something."

"You're saying running into a weird door that suddenly appears at the back of the library isn't suspicious? This was never here before. I would have noticed it. I've spent a lot of time in the spell section."

"No, it *is* suspicious. But so was the blood on your shoes." I pointed down at his now-clean toes. "You had those on the day Kendra was found, and they were covered in blood splatters."

"Are you saying you still think I—"

"No! I'm saying we need more to go on than a coincidence or a smell or whatever."

Gavin sighed and shoved his adorably floppy hair out of his face. "You're right. We have to get inside the door. I'm betting whatever's back there, it has something to do with the attacks. It's definitely got magical properties."

"How can you tell?"

"Look." He grabbed me by the shoulders and turned me around to face the wall where the door was. "It's already fading into the plaster. You can only see the outline of the handle."

"Whoa. Sinister." I was suddenly very glad we *hadn't* been able to get inside and follow the person in black. Call me crazy, but I didn't want to be trapped behind some magical door with a potential psychopath. At least not without some sort of weapon. Preferably a large, blunt object good for bashing a brain-thief's head in. "Is there a tool shed anywhere around here? Or a janitor's closet? I want to get my hands on a hammer or something before we try to get in there."

"I can get you something better than a hammer. My roommate has a mace collection Samedi missed during her inspection." I turned around to see Gavin staring at me with a rather pleased smile on his face. If I didn't know better, I'd think he was proud of my bloodthirsty nature.

But then ... did I *really* know better? For all I knew, Gavin could enjoy torturing small animals in his spare time. I didn't think he was the brain thief anymore, but that didn't mean he didn't have violent tendencies. If I were smart, I would keep my head on my shoulders until I got to know this guy and not be swept away by his yumminess. Good-looking, charming people could still be evil. (Just look at my little sister Kimmy—gorgeous and gregarious, yet never happier than when tormenting my brothers and breaking their Handy Manny toys.)

"And don't worry, I won't let anything happen to you this time." Gavin took one of my hands in his and squeezed. My head promptly fell right off my shoulders. How could I think logically when he was standing so close and holding my hand? *Holding my hand.* Geez, who would have thought mere hand-holding could be so fabulous? "I promise I'll be prepared to fight back. Just give me until after sixth period to figure a few things out, and I'll let you know the plan."

"Okay." I nodded, refusing to give in to the fear tickling along my skin and doing its best to banish the hand-holding thrill. I wasn't going to chicken out now, not when it seemed we finally had something worth investigating.

"You want to have dinner together? Get our own table?"

"Sure, that would be cool," I said nonchalantly, as if cute boys held my hand and asked me for private meals on a daily basis. "Easier to plan that way. We don't want anyone to hear what we're up to."

"Totally." He smiled at me again, a sort of checking-out-the-Karen smile that made me want to fidget or wipe my face to make sure there wasn't anything gross and crusty stuck on the sides of my lips, but I didn't do either. I just stood there, staring back at him, waiting ... for something. What, I didn't know. But there was *something* about to happen. I could just *feel* it.

When he spoke again, it was in this husky whisper that tripped so many girl reactions within me at once that it was impossible to give his words any meaning. I honestly had no idea what he'd said, only that he'd moved his lips and pretty sounds had come out.

"Um, what?" I asked, my voice scratchier than I'd ever heard it.

"I said, that wasn't blood on my shoes. It was paint." His face moved slowly closer to mine, for reasons my muddled brain couldn't comprehend. Surely he wasn't going to ... he wouldn't ... not right here ... not right now! I mean, I'd secretly been hoping, but I'd never really thought... "I suck at art."

"Oh. Yeah?"

"Yeah. I always drop stuff."

"Yeah ... stuff." My lips parted a little without my really thinking about it. It was just an instinctive response to Gavin's peppermint-scented breath against my skin, to the feel of his brain-warmed flesh getting closer and closer to my own.

There was no doubt about it now. Gavin was going to kiss me. Gavin. Was going to. Kiss. *Me!* Within mere seconds, lip-locking would no longer be a fantasy but a—

"Miss Vera. Mr. McDougal." The sharp bark of the voice was topped only by the sharper bark of his cologne. Argh! Mr. Cork! What were the freaking *odds*? "You'll need to come with me. Immediately."

Gavin and I leapt apart with identical guilty looks. I was blushing with a heat that I'd been unaware Undead flesh could achieve, and I doubted I would ever be able to look Mr. Cork in his sunken eyes again. Gavin, however, recovered rather quickly.

"Mr. Cork! I was just helping Karen with some homework. It's her first week and—"

"I am well aware it is Miss Vera's first week at school. And that she has missed an astounding amount of class for any DEAD student, let alone one who should be doing her utmost to catch up with her peers." Mr. Cork pointed a single bony finger back toward the library's entrance. "The bell signaling the end of lunch rang a good five minutes past. Both of you are *tardy*. I'll need you to follow me."

Coming out of Mr. Cork's mouth, "tardy" sounded like something akin to "baby killer" or "kitten drowner." There was clearly no worse sin we could have committed, which made me hopeful that he wouldn't mention anything about the near-kiss he'd observed. I couldn't claim to be an expert in boys, but I guessed being publicly humiliated for almost kissing someone was a good way for that someone to *never* get almost kissed again.

And I really wanted to be almost kissed. Or, better yet, just flat-out kissed. It didn't seem right to keep risking my life trying to catch a brain thief with something as important as my first kiss still unfinished.

Still, I couldn't even look at Gavin as we trudged out of the library behind Mr. Cork. I'd faced a lot of scary things in the past few days, but I wasn't quite up to meeting the electric blue eyes of the cutest boy in the entire world less than two minutes post-aborted lip-lock.

———

Come dinner, Gavin was nowhere to be found, making me wonder if maybe Principal Samedi *was* behind all the dastardly doings after all. She'd intercepted us on the way to the office and, after a little whispered meeting with Cork, relieved him of our teenaged selves, all too happy to take the disciplining into her own hands.

Miraculously, I'd gotten off with a stern warning not to be late to any more classes, but Gavin hadn't been so lucky. She'd kept him prisoner in her office while I'd been forced to scurry off to class under the care of an armed guard. The halls were swarming with them now, tons of men and women in camo gear glaring at the student-filled halls like they were crawling with snipers.

It would have made me feel better about Samedi's commitment to preserving our health and brains if I didn't suspect she'd done something awful to Gavin. He'd looked pretty pale when I'd left. Definitely in fear for his life. Poor guy.

"Menu?" the red-haired girl on duty asked, somehow

managing to make the one-word question sound like an insult to my entire family line.

Geez. Could I get a little more beloved by my peers?

"Sure." I took the menu and eased off to the side of the line of students headed into the cafeteria, faking a moment of rabid indecision about whether to go raw or cooked while I searched the crowd one more time for my dinner date.

Menu Friday Dinner

The raw line:
Emu brains and ground emu thigh stew
with a side of salmon eggs.

The hot line:
Organic pig brains on multigrain flat bread,
topped with a cow brain and garlic, non-dairy remoulade.

Remoulade? What exactly *was* a remoulade?

While I was pondering the wisdom of eating something I couldn't pronounce, my evil roommate slunk around me in a cloud of her own foul breath. She didn't even bother with her usual half-grunted "hi," which was pretty weird considering we hadn't seen each other in days. Every time I'd been in our room, she'd been MIA. I'd assumed she was shacking up with her friend Darby, whose roommate had gone home after Kendra's attack. (Seemed some parents still loved their Undead children enough to pull them out of school when people's brains started getting snatched.)

Under normal circumstances, I would have gladly allowed Clarice to avoid me, but I needed to get close to her and this might be my only chance.

"Clarice, wait up," I said, hurrying after her as she took her place at the end of the raw line. Emu it was. Weird, but at least it wasn't topped with something scary and French-sounding.

Clarice heaved a sigh that made it clear I was a curse upon her existence. "What do you want?"

"I was just ... wondering where you were sitting." I sidled up to her, getting as close as I possibly could and taking a deep breath. My gag reflex threatened to engage as Clarice's stank breath violated my nose in ten different ways, but somehow I managed to keep my friendly smile in place and my dried brain bar in my stomach.

"You've got to be kidding me."

"Nope, I don't kid. Not much of a kidder." I smiled, a grin perky enough to melt even Clarice's cold heart ... at least a little bit. She didn't smile back, but she did at least consent to give me a civil answer.

"Sorry. I'm sitting with Darby, and there's not going to be room for you." She tried to spin around, but I darted forward before she could give me the frigid goth shoulder.

"Oh, that's too bad." I struggled to think of something else to say to keep her talking. My analysis of her stank vs. the stank Gavin and I had encountered in the library was as yet inconclusive. I needed more time! "So, how are your classes going?"

Clarice gave me a look almost eloquent in its expression of supreme disdain. "Why are you still talking? Are you, like, brain damaged or something, Pink?"

"Um...yeah. Guess so." I retreated with a little wave, amid snorts of amusement from the popular junior girls standing in front of Clarice. They even spared a smile for her as she turned around. I tried to feel good about the fact that hatred of Karen Vera was uniting the people, but I just couldn't. In fact, it was all I could do not to start crying.

So far I'd kept a pretty stiff upper lip about being judged and misunderstood, but it hurt. A lot. Especially when I thought about my old life, when I'd had more friends than I could count on two hands and people only hated me because I was more popular than they were or got to stand at the top of the pyramid instead of having my shoulders stomped on and covered in cleat bruises.

I'd assumed the shame of the moment couldn't get any worse, but seconds later I was knocked flat on the ground as a large, solid mass of Undead flesh shoved past me in line. I looked up to see an absolutely *enormous* girl, with damp dirty-blond hair cut in an unflattering pageboy, standing next to Clarice. (Our teacher for *Secrets of Morticians*, Ms. Klein, was also a licensed beautician and gave free haircuts to DEAD students on Friday afternoons, so there was no excuse for such a hatchet job.)

I was trying to think of a nonchalant way to clue this chick in to the fashion aid available at her fingertips when she wrinkled her pug nose in my direction. As *if* I could smell one fifth as bad as Clarice's breath.

"Oh, sorry." But she didn't sound sorry. At all. "Hope you don't mind if I cut."

The popular girls giggled again, and one deigned to talk to the new arrival. "Hey, Darby."

So *this* was Darby. This enormous, muscular chick, with man-hands big and strong enough to hold a smaller girl immobilized while she hacked open her victim's skull. What if she was the brawn and Clarice the brains? If they were working together, there was no doubt Clarice had the muscle power to get the harvesting job done.

And if I wasn't mistaken, this Darby chick smelled distinctly of chlorine. The pool had been closed until further notice, so why had she been taking a pre-dinner dip? There was something fishy going on.

Seeing as Gavin was nowhere to be found, I figured I might as well try to get a bead on the Clarice and Darby thing. I still wasn't sure if Clarice's stench was *the* stench, but Darby had more than aroused my curiosity. And suspicion.

Doing my best to fade into the background, I trailed the other girls through the raw line and slunk to an isolated table not too far from where my roommate and her man-hand friend were settling down to a very cozy chat. Something was *definitely* up. I couldn't hear what they were saying, but Darby kept sneaking nervous looks at the rest of the cafeteria, and Clarice looked like she'd gotten her Celebration of the Dark Lord's Birth presents early. (I was betting she didn't do Christmas.)

The two of them were so freaking obvious in their evil plotting that I wasn't even surprised when Darby pulled a tiny silver chain out of her pocket and slipped it across the table to Clarice. I wasn't close enough to be sure, but I was betting money that it was Trish's chain, the one with the little sterling silver scorpion to celebrate her Scorpio-ness.

Had Darby gone diving in the pool to look for it? If so, why? What could she possibly want with a victim's necklace?

Argh! I needed Gavin. If it was some sort of magic thing, he'd know about it and—

"Hey, sorry I'm late." As if summoned by my thoughts, Gavin appeared at my table. He looked a little frazzled and hadn't bothered to get a tray, but that didn't matter. I was still so happy to see him it was hard to keep any portion of my attention on my suspects.

"No big deal." I smiled and did my best to keep my eyes from wandering to the lips that I had come *sooooo* close to kissing. "I'm just glad you're okay. I thought Samedi had you for dinner."

He grimaced and swallowed hard. "Yeah, about that. I'm not going to be able to have dinner with you tonight."

"Oh. Well, that's okay, maybe we can meet during rec hours or—"

"You don't get it," he said, frustration simmering beneath every word. "We're not going to meet anywhere. Not for dinner, not during rec hours, not ever."

"But … I thought—"

"You thought I'd be into a dumb cheerleader? Well, I'm not." He backed away, his voice rising until I knew the entire cafeteria could hear him. "I'm not interested, Karen. So stay the hell away from me." Seconds later he was gone, spinning on his heel and ambling over to the hot line as if he hadn't just ruined my life.

My mouth fell open and I think I made some sort of gagging sound, but I couldn't be sure. All I knew was that every eye in the room was trained on my face, watching the tears pool in my eyes with smiles of satisfaction. And laughter. They were laughing at my complete humiliation, eating up my pain like I was covered in freaking remoulade.

With a sob, I pushed back my chair and dashed for the exit, not even bothering to put away my tray. I didn't care if I followed the rules at this stupid school. I just wanted out. Away from the brains and the death and the zombie kids who gave new meaning to the word "evil." Anyone who thought trying to munch your flesh was the worst thing a zombie could do was so wrong. What these creeps did was way worse. At least flesh-eating zombies were just stupid and hungry. They didn't enjoy watching someone suffer.

I had to stop running before I'd gone very far. I was crying too hard to see where I was going, and the last thing I needed was another injury. If I was going to make it back to my parents' house, I had to stay in one piece. Of course, I probably should have eaten my wretched food, no matter how miserable I was. Who knew how long it would take me to find a steady supply of brains up in Peachtree? Call me crazy, but I didn't think it was something I could just add to Mom's Trader Joe's list next to formula and recycled diapers.

"No way, we can't wait. We'll have to go now, or it will be too late." The hushed voice was coming from around the corner, giving me just enough time to duck into the classroom behind me before I was spotted. Luckily, the door had a narrow glass window, and I was just barely tall enough to peek through the bottom.

"I don't know. That's some serious magic. Do you think you can handle it?" It was Darby, with a very excited Clarice by her side.

"Of course I can. You saw what happened in the caf-eteria, right?" Clarice laughed. "I thought everyone was going to jump on her and rip her apart with their teeth."

Darby smiled but still looked a little worried. "Yeah, but that's just a personal hex. This could be—"

"This could be great. Exactly what we've been dream-ing about! Come on, don't be a baby. I thought you were into this?"

"I am." Darby sighed the sigh of the peer-pressured, but I didn't feel sorry for her. I might not know much about magic, but I could put the phrases "personal hex" and "jump on her and rip her apart with their teeth" together and come up with a theory.

Clarice had been hexing *me*, and Darby knew all

about it. My own roommate had been doing her best to make sure I was hated by the entire school! It was such a relief to realize I hadn't suddenly become the most unlikable person on the planet—and maybe Gavin didn't really think I was the human embodiment of pond scum—but still! Argh! What a witch! If I wasn't pretty sure she'd also snatched Trish's brain, I would have jumped Clarice right there and shown her what cheerleader muscles could do to her face.

But I couldn't seek my own vengeance just yet. I had to follow these two freaks and see if they led me to the harvested brains—before it was too late.

THIRTEEN

Using magic against another student—particularly black magic—will result in immediate suspension and possible expulsion from DEAD High. If the accused individual is convicted of dabbling in the dark arts, he or she will be barred from DEAD and all Death Challenged educational institutions and have both of his/her hands cut off at the wrist as per High Council edict 25. Remember, casting with intent to harm is a criminal offense, not merely against school policy.

—*School Handbook, DEAD High*

Don't mess with the darkness, don't mess with it
    man,
don't mess with the darkness or they'll take your
    hand, your evil, no-good casting hand.

—*"Don't Mess with the Darkness," by the
Scatterbrains, Top 40 Undead Hits of the 1960s*

Libraries have to be one of the safest places on earth. They're so quiet and filled with books and nice, quiet people who like to read books. (And homeless people, but they usually keep a lid on it when they're in the library and save all the crazy ranting stuff for out on the street, which is cool of them.) Libraries are safe, homey public places, unlike post offices, which gave me the creeps even before I was old enough understand the whole "going postal" thing.

But tonight... the school library was a bona fide creepfest.

I could feel the evil floating in the room the second I slipped through the door after Clarice and Darby. There was something awful going down in this usually cozy space. The air was so thick with bad vibes that it hurt to breathe and my skin started to itch.

I was so unnerved, it was nearly impossible to dash past the front desk and crouch down behind the computer study station, but I did it. Trish and Penelope and Kendra were counting on me. Clarice seemed determined to work whatever spell she and Darby had been planning tonight, which meant three precious brains were on the verge of being forever beyond redemption.

Hushed whispers from behind the rows of books led me to the exact same spot where Gavin and I had seen the figure in black disappear earlier in the day. Clarice was busy at the wall and seemed to know just what to do to summon the scary door from its hiding place. She whispered a few words, and seconds later the red-eyed snakes were visible even from several feet away.

These two just kept looking guiltier and guiltier... and I kept getting more and more freaked. I had to stay close so I could slip through the door after them, but I *really* didn't want to take another step toward that side of the room.

The evil was coming from that door—waves of pure nasty that oozed across my skin, raising every little blond hair and making me feel like I had to … pee.

Oh … no! I *really* did have to pee. Like, *badly*.

What was I going to do?! It wasn't like I could call a time-out for a bathroom break.

Crap! This *never* happened to crime fighters in movies or books. Why had I been cursed with the smallest bladder on the planet? How was I going to tell Trish's heartbroken single mother that I'd failed to recover her daughter's brain because I had to *go make tinkle*?

I spun around, planning a mad dash to the girls' toilet just outside the library, and ran straight into a wall of boy.

"Oof," I grunted as I bounced off of Gavin and hit the ground with an audible plop.

Crap again! Surely Clarice and Darby had heard me. I froze, straining to hear the sounds of the two harvesters rushing my way, but the library was silent.

"What are you doing here?" Gavin hissed, reaching a hand down to help me to my feet.

"Shh!" I held a finger to my lips, thankful my moment of panic seemed to have banished the bathroom emergency. "Clarice and Darby are—"

"They're already inside the door, and I would be too if you had listened to me."

I snatched my hand from his and stuck my nose higher

in the air than was probably reasonable or attractive. "You told me you didn't want to hang out. I don't remember anything about not following suspects to the library. Besides, who made you my boss?"

Gavin ran a frustrated hand through his hair and made a sound somewhere between a growl and a sigh. "You've got to get out of here. It's not safe." He tried to grab me by the shoulders but I slipped away. Cute or not, I was not going to let him manhandle me. Or boyhandle me, or whatever.

Besides, I hadn't forgiven him for what he'd said to me in the cafeteria. Even though I knew he was probably under Clarice's evil spell, those words had hurt. A lot.

"I'm going to get through that door and help Trish. That's the only place I'm going," I insisted, standing my ground. "I heard Clarice and Darby talking about working a spell tonight. They're the ones responsible for—"

"No, they're not. Principal Samedi is. She knows I've been dabbling with magic." He cast a worried look over his shoulder, like he feared the woman in question might have tailed him to the library. "This afternoon she threatened to expel me or worse."

"Or worse? What does that mean?"

"Use your imagination," he said, shifting nervously from foot to foot, making me wonder if scary libraries made him have to pee too. "I was getting a really bad vibe, so I didn't go back to class. I waited until she left her office and followed her. Guess where she went?"

"Into the door." My stomach sank when Gavin nodded.

"But not before grabbing something from her private kitchen. Something that had to be kept in a cooler." He looked nervously around the library once more before easing toward the door. "I'll give you three guesses what she had in there, and the first two don't count."

"Oh god. The brains?"

"I'm guessing. And I think she saw me following her. Or felt me or something. So I didn't want you coming with me tonight." He cleared his throat. "I thought the...thing in the cafeteria would keep you away from me."

"You could have just asked." I stepped to the side as Gavin patted the wall down, supposedly looking for some sign of where the door had gone.

"You wouldn't have listened."

"No, I wouldn't have." I was surprised that he knew me so well after only a few days. "But at least I would have been spared embarrassment on a tragic scale. That was...awful."

"I'm sorry," he said, sounding truly remorseful. "But I was trying to make sure no one thought you were helping me investigate." He turned his attention away from the door and stepped a little closer to me, treating me to a whiff of the yummy, soapy boy smell that was Gavin. "Otherwise I wouldn't have...you know? I was just trying to make sure everyone thought we were broken up so they wouldn't think—"

"Broken up?" I was pretty sure my eyebrows shot up to touch my scalp. "I didn't know we were...I mean...I never...yeah..."

Gavin actually blushed. Blushed! Red enough so that I could see it even in the near darkness. "Well, there were rumors. I didn't start them or anything, but...yeah...I mean...it's cool."

It's cool. Did that mean he thought that him and me, together, could be cool? OMG. I could be seconds away from having a boyfriend, a real boyfriend! Gavin didn't just like me, he *liked* me. But if he had been faking his hatred...

"So you weren't under a voodoo hex that made you hate me?" Geez, did all my theories have to be blown to heck mere *minutes* after I had conceived them? And more importantly, was Gavin going to say anything else about these dating rumors and their coolness?

"Um...not that I know of."

"Ugh, that sucks."

"I can try to hex myself if you want."

"No, it's not—it's just that—" Blerck! This was not coming out the way I wanted it to at all. Why was I suddenly so socially dysfunctional? This never would have happened in my old life.

"You know what? We don't have time to talk about it right now." He seemed irritated again as he turned back to the wall. Great. Now we were probably on the verge of breaking up before I even had the chance to figure out if Gavin wanted to be together. "We have to get in that door."

"You're right." And he was. We had to stay focused, or brains and lives were going to be lost. There would be time to angst out about us (OMG, please let there still be an *us*!) later. "Whether it's Samedi or Clarice and Darby, I don't think Trish and the others have much time. Something's going down tonight. I can just feel it."

"I know, I—" He broke off with an excited smile. If I didn't know better I'd think a part of him was enjoying this. But then, I guess a part of me was too. We totally shared the crime fighter gene and would probably grow up and work in Special Ops together or something even cooler. "I think I found it."

Keeping one hand on a spot on the wall, he pulled a tangled root out of his robe pocket with the other. He chanted a few words I thought were in French—"remoulade" might have been in there somewhere—and then traced the root along the plaster in the shape of the door. Seconds later, the wall began to glow a faint blue and the snake door appeared, looking as ominous and foreboding as it had the first time. "You ready?" he asked, his hand shaking a little as he grabbed the handle.

"Ready," I nodded, though I really wished I'd made time to find that hammer. I would have felt a lot better following Gavin through a spooky door and down an even spookier set of damp, moldy stairs if I'd had a nice, heavy hammer in hand.

Or a gun would have been good. I'd never even *seen* a gun before in real life, since my parents were very anti-firearm, but how hard could shooting a gun be? I think I could figure out how to turn off the safety and blast a hole in someone who was trying to steal my brain. I'm not a violent person, but given the choice between them and me, I'm picking me. Especially if *they* are a brain snatcher and *I* am not.

"Hold on to me," Gavin whispered over his shoulder. I gladly obliged, grabbing a handful of the back of his uniform.

It was getting *really* dark as we descended the stairs, making me wish I had one of those big industrial flashlights. Not only would it be good for seeing, but those things are really heavy. Almost as good as a hammer, really. Not as good as a gun, but—

"Karen? Did you hear me?"

"No, sorry," I said, struggling to focus. Thinking about weapons wasn't going to make one magically appear. My best weapon right now was paying attention and being ready to run if I had to.

"I thought I heard something," he whispered as I tottered off the final step behind him, just barely keeping my balance in the utter blackness. Geez! How did Darby and Clarice get so far ahead of us so fast? Clarice was clearly part serpent and could see in the dark, but Darby *must* have had problems. "But I can't tell where it's coming from. I think we can go either right or left. There's a wall directly in front."

I felt him groping around in the darkness and tightened my grip on his robe. I didn't want to get separated down here. Gavin was right, the sound was all wonky and seemed to be coming from everywhere at once. It was hard to pinpoint the direction of his voice and he was standing right in front of me. If I lost contact, I might never find him again.

"I think right," I finally whispered, knowing my heart would be pounding a million miles a minute if it could still beat.

It was awful down here. The evil vibe actually wasn't quite as bad as it had been in the library, but everything still felt … wrong. It reminded me of the *Alice and Wonderland* cartoon where she falls through the rabbit hole and lands upside down. I wouldn't be at all surprised if the lights were to suddenly flare on and Gavin and I found ourselves standing on the ceiling.

"I think I see a light." I squinted until my eyes hurt, trying to pinpoint the source.

"Yeah … sort of red."

"And scary." I stepped closer and grabbed another handful of robe with my other fist as Gavin turned and began shuffling toward the light. I felt sort of like a baby monkey clinging to its mother's fur, which was probably not cool. But then, being cooler than a monkey was the least of my worries right now.

The smell was back, slinking down the dark tunnel ahead of us, pungent and rotten, a school bully that grabbed hold of your face and stuck it deep in his nasty armpit. I thought I heard Gavin gag a little, which made me want to gag too, but I shoved the urge away. Bent double, yacking your guts out, was not a good position to be found in if you happened to attract the attention of a brain harvester.

And we were totally going to attract attention. Surely these other people had some sort of magic or something that helped them see down here in the pit—and surely they would notice us coming. Then they'd leap out from the blackness and hack our skulls open with a garden trowel or a kitchen knife or something blunter that would hurt even more!

Stop it! Think positively! Positive winner thoughts.

The inner voice was right. First law of cheering: you have to stay cheer-full, filled with positive energy. It is a scientifically proven fact that negative vibes from the sidelines can alter the course of an entire game and prevent any hopes of a comeback on the part of the home team.

I never would have dared to think loser thoughts while in my official PHS Peachpit Pride cheer uniform. I wasn't going to start thinking loser thoughts now, either, even if the scene coming into view was the definition of disturbing.

Not more than thirty feet away, figures in black hooded robes stood in a circle around a small stone altar that was surrounded by writhing black snakes with glowing red eyes. There were at least a hundred snakes churning around the stone, hissing when they drew too close to the unnaturally bright red fire that burned there. The fire was the color of melted cherry jawbreakers and red neon mixed together and was fueled by nothing other than … brains. Real, live … er, *dead*, brains.

I slammed a hand over my mouth to stifle the horror-movie-heroine shriek trying to escape my lips and fought the urge to run. This was way more alarming than anything I'd imagined.

Snakes are not my favorite critters, not by a long shot, and the brains seemed...alive. All three pulsed and throbbed upon the altar, like they were still capable of thought and ached to be back in the skulls where they belonged. Their slick gray surfaces squirmed as the fire grew higher and higher, and I knew they would totally have been screaming for mercy if they'd had mouths to scream with.

It was an awful thing to see, and—if my guess was right—it was also the source of the horrible smell. Though now that we were closer, the smell had changed a bit. It was more of a rancid-barbeque-pit kind of stink rather than the sickeningly sweet rot of a few moments before.

No, wait—the rotted smell was still there, but it had shifted somehow. Now it seemed to be coming from behind us. Maybe we'd passed a dead animal or something in the tunnel and just hadn't realized it. (Ew! Tunnel kill, very, very gross.)

But then again, a dead animal wouldn't slowly be drawing closer, giving the barbeque-from-hell smell a run for its money. And a dead animal wouldn't have a slightly familiar, human scent, something I couldn't quite put my finger on but that reminded me of something...of some-one. God, what was that? That faint spicy smell that made my flesh crawl and the place between my shoulders scream for me to hit the deck?

I had to ask Gavin if he smelled it too, even if it meant risking being overheard.

I tugged softly on his robe. "Gavin, do you—"

"Grab them! Don't let them leave the circle!"

Oh crap! We'd been discovered! Principal Samedi had never sounded so scary. I was guessing the echo had something to do with it, but still—whoa, had she ever been holding back on Gavin and me in her office. If we'd known how spooky that voice could get, we never would have dared follow her through the hallways, let alone down into her secret sacrificial lair.

Her shout was terrifying enough to bring my urge to pee surging back with a vengeance, but I ignored it. There was no time to stress about small bladders and bathroom breaks. Gavin and I had to get the heck out of there. We had to run for it and hope we could reach the human world before Samedi caught up with us. DEAD was on the outskirts of Atlanta, in a mostly industrial district, but there *had* to be humans around somewhere. And surely Principal Samedi wouldn't dare harvest our brains with normal people around to observe.

But if she was psycho enough to cut out brains in the first place, who knew what she would do? And with magic like hers, she could probably work a spell to make sure a normal human never remembered they'd encountered two teenagers on the run from a murderer.

Or maybe she'd just kill them and us and be done with it.

I yanked harder on Gavin's robe. "Come on! We have to—"

Gavin's hand came down over my eyes, then slid down my nose to cover my mouth. "Shh!" He pulled me with him as he smashed flat against the wall. We'd just disappeared into the shadows when Darby and Clarice raced by, breathing heavily enough that I could smell the telltale stank of Clarice's breath.

Seconds later, three of the hooded figures, carrying torches, raced after the girls, pursuing them down the tunnel. I felt Gavin relax against me as they disappeared into the darkness, and experienced a similar moment of relief. We hadn't been spotted after all. It was Darby and Clarice who were going to have their entrails ripped out for daring to interrupt Samedi's brain spell.

Said relief lasted all of thirty seconds before a claw-like hand clamped down on my shoulder, and Gavin and I both screamed. Our heads snapped up in tandem, so I knew he was seeing exactly what I was seeing—Principal Samedi, hanging from the ceiling like some sort of bat, her spiky black hair forming horns that framed her psychotically pissed-off face.

FOURTEEN

I did what none of you had the guts to do, losers.
You're just a bunch of sheep! A bunch of sheep!
Fight the power. Fight the freaking power!

—*Allan Yarborough, upon the occasion of his*
suspension from DEAD High

The boy just disappeared off the face of the earth.
We searched for him ourselves and alerted the
national Patrollers, but he was never found. We can
only assume he met with some sort of unfortunate
accident.

—*Principal Samedi, upon the occasion of her*
questioning by the school board on the mysterious
disappearance of Allan Yarborough

Monkey brains. It had been monkey brains on the altar.

Actually, baboon brains, which were extremely difficult to acquire and illegal in several states, but Samedi swore they'd been taken from baboons who had died of natural causes. They'd been purchased from a wildlife refuge instead of the more affordable poacher channels and had cost the school nearly three thousand dollars apiece.

That was *nine thousand dollars* down the drain because Clarice and Darby had violated the circle Principal Samedi and her coven members had cast. (Gavin and I would have done the same thing if we'd walked further down the hall, so we were in just as deep doo as my roommate and her partner in crime.)

"But you've cost us more than money tonight," Principal Samedi said, her voice thick with disappointment. She leaned over her desk, glaring first into my eyes, then into Gavin's. I swear I could feel my corneas starting to smolder.

Gavin and I both sank a little deeper in our chairs. Clarice and Darby had already taken their medicine and been escorted out of the office a few minutes ago. I'd been glad they were yelled at first, but now I'd changed my mind. I wished more than anything that this was over.

Samedi wasn't about to let up. "You've cost us our best chance at finding the harvested brains of your three classmates before it's too late to reunite them with their bodies." Her hands were still claw-shaped and made scary scratching sounds on her desk as she drummed her nails.

She hadn't given any explanation as to how she was able to hang from the ceiling, and Gavin and I hadn't asked. I didn't know about him, but I was now properly afraid of my new principal and didn't want to do anything else to hack her off.

"We were just trying to help." Gavin was actually looking her in the eye as he spoke, proving he had way more guts than I'd ever have. "We saw Darby and Clarice going through the door in the library and—"

"Darby and Clarice are not now and have never been your responsibility. You are a student here at DEAD, Mr. McDougal. You are not in a position of power and—"

"And I don't want to be." Gavin's voice rose. What was he doing? Didn't he realize we were in deep trouble already? "Don't you think I'd rather let the alleged adults around here handle this? Don't you think I want to believe you've got the safety of the school under control? Well, I would, but you don't."

"That's enough, Gavin." Principal Samedi snapped the words with her usual toughness, but it was too late. I'd seen the crack in her confidence, and Gavin had obviously seen it too, because he didn't hesitate for a second before driving his argument home.

"You don't, or Darby and Clarice would never have been able to follow you. They never would have been able to get Trish's necklace or even *think* they could get away with tracking down—"

"I said, that's *enough*. You don't—"

"No, it's not enough." I winced as he jumped to his feet. Gah! This was going to end badly. Why couldn't he just quit while he was ahead? "What about the hex Clarice put on Karen?"

In other news, Clarice had confessed to hexing me. Samedi and her coven had searched our room and found a bunch of my stuff mixed in with her chicken bone collection. It was a particularly nasty personal hex spell that would have been even more damaging if she'd been able to get her hands on human bones. No word yet as to *why* she'd decided to make me her victim, but apparently that's what she'd been up to while she was hiding under her blanket with *my* Hello Kitty flashlight.

I was so going to *insist* on a new roommate, no excuses accepted...if Clarice and I weren't both expelled.

"Clarice will be dealt with," Principal Samedi said in her soft, scary voice. She was doing her best to get this situation under control, but I could tell she kind of wanted to leap across the desk and strangle Gavin.

"Yeah, now she will be, but what about before? Didn't you even notice that the entire school was treating the new girl like shit for no reason?"

OMG, Gavin had just cussed. In front of the principal. This was going past "has guts" into "has a death wish" territory. The woman was part vampire bat or something, for god's sake. What did he think he was doing?

"And if I hadn't already done something to protect myself from the rogue magic at this school, I would have been affected too." Gavin pulled his gris-gris bag out from under his robe. It contained a bunch of herbs and stuff and served as a talisman to ward off evil. Gavin had promised to make me one as soon as we were released from custody. "I shouldn't have to work protection spells to keep myself safe from black magic."

Samedi sighed and dropped her eyes to her hands—which were looking a little less clawlike. Thank god. The whole channeling-a-batlike-creature thing was very whiggy. "No, you shouldn't have to. And I'm sorry."

Holy. Crackers. And. Cheese. She'd just apologized. I couldn't believe it, but it looked like Gavin had won this argument.

"There have been ... challenges for the administration," Samedi added slowly. "And for me in particular."

"What kind of challenges?" Gavin asked, easing back into his chair.

"I'm not at liberty to share that information, but suffice it to say that these challenges have kept me from performing my duties as principal with the excellence I would prefer. And for that, I apologize." Samedi looked first at me and then at Gavin, her dark eyes so sad I couldn't help but feel a little sorry for her.

"Still, the division of my attention couldn't be helped. I've done what I've thought was best for the school in the past week." She rose from her chair and crossed to a cabinet on the other side of the room. "You'll just have to trust that I have been doing all I could to provide for the safety of not only yourselves, but the entire student body. My worst mistake was underestimating the determination and curiosity of my students, but I assure you, that won't happen again."

She turned back to us, a small black bottle in her hand. "Until the situation that arose this evening is under control, anyone violating school policy will be suspended until further notice."

"You wouldn't dare." Gavin stood up so quickly his chair fell over with a loud clatter. "That's against the law."

"Gavin, I don't think it's against the law for Principal Samedi to suspend us," I said, trying to talk some sense into him before he got himself expelled or something worse. "She *is* the principal and we did break the—"

"She's not going to suspend us from school, she's going to put us under a suspension spell. Suspended animation." Gavin grabbed my hand and pulled me to my feet beside him before turning back to Samedi. "It's black magic to freeze another person in time against their will, and black magic is against the law. For everyone."

"Technically, it's gray magic, and in times of crisis we do what we must." Samedi uncorked the bottle in her hand. "I'm truly sorry, but I don't feel you've given me any choice."

"Run, Karen!" Gavin spun on his heel and bolted for the door, dragging me with him.

"But I—"

"Run!"

I turned to race after him, just barely making it through the office door before an explosion of blue light erupted behind me. Yikes! I wasn't sure if that was the suspended animation spell, but it certainly packed a punch. I could feel crackles of electricity sparking along my skin, singeing little blond hairs. And that was just from being close to the thing.

"Come on, this way," Gavin shouted, hauling serious butt down the hall to the right.

I pulled up the hem of my robe and pumped my legs

as hard as I could to keep up, even though I still wasn't sure if this was the right thing to do. Being frozen in time didn't sound like much fun, but what choice did we have? We couldn't run from Principal Samedi forever. Where were we going to go? My earlier plan to run and hide among the human population would only work for so long. Samedi would eventually find us and work her magic or use her claws to rip us open and eat our entrails or whatever else she was in the mood to do at the time. We had to get *real* help, someone inside the Death Challenged community who would offer us protection. But who could we turn to who would believe Samedi had gone off the deep end?

"This way!" A low, gravelly voice sounded from our right.

Gavin and I both yelled as a skeletal hand closed around our arms and yanked us into an abandoned room at the end of the hall. The door slammed seconds later amidst a cloud of pungent cologne. It was Mr. Cork, looking even worse than usual. His skin hung on him like a deflated balloon, and his dark brown eyes glittered unhealthily in his sunken face.

"Both of you, follow me. We haven't much time." Mr. Cork shuffled to the corner of the room, every movement looking like an exercise in pain. "Samedi won't let you escape. Not after all you've seen."

"Those weren't baboon brains, were they?" Gavin asked, pulling me across the room as Cork went to work on the wall with a root, summoning a black door much like the one we'd slipped through in the library. Except this one didn't have snakes on it, but pudgy, white wormy things. Ick. They were gross looking, but not particularly scary. If we were to encounter a writhing pile of white worms on the other side of that door, I figured we could probably survive the experience.

"No, they were not. Theresa has crossed the line into black magic and refuses to come back to the light," Mr. Cork said, grunting and wheezing with the effort it took to speak. "I discovered the harvested brains in her laboratory and tried to convince her to abandon her wicked plan, but she will not be swayed. She tried to kill me for what I knew, and she'll do the same to both of you. Clarice and Darby have already disappeared. I doubt their bodies will ever be found."

Oh … crap. This was exceptionally bad news. For all practical purposes, I knew I should have been having a full-on panic attack as I waited for the frail Mr. Cork to open the door. I could hear Principal Samedi looking for us, her heeled boots clicking on the tile outside as she hurried down the hall. We were probably seconds away from death by arm-hair-singeing blue light. But for some reason … I wasn't scared. Not of Principal Samedi, at least.

Something else *was* bothering me. Something I couldn't quite put my finger on.

"Heeled boots. She always wears heeled boots," I said, tugging on Gavin's robe. "And she's not heavy enough to make those footsteps we heard at the pool or I heard in the bathroom. It can't be her. At least not only her."

"She's probably working with one of the people from her coven," Gavin said, just as Mr. Cork pulled the door open.

It swung into the room with a creaking sound and a puff of stale air. Wherever this door led, it hadn't been opened in a long time. I peeked past Gavin to see a dusty brown corridor decorated with strange markings along both walls that seemed to stretch on into infinity. At first glance, it was much less creepy than the moldy stairs we'd trudged down earlier in the night, but for some reason I *really* didn't want to go into that hallway.

The evil aura that had been lurking around the library seethed out of the brown stones ahead of us, shoving out into the room, clutching at my throat like a big, invisible fist. It got harder and harder to breathe every second I stared through the door, making me dig my heels in and hold my ground when Gavin tried to pull me forward.

"Wait, I don't think—"

"Come on, Karen. She's almost here!" The panic in Gavin's eyes made me take a step closer, against my will. He was the experienced magical person—surely he would know if we were headed into a bad-juju zone.

"Hurry. I won't be able to protect either of you. I'm too weak." Mr. Cork stepped up behind me, his jumbo-soled heels making a thumping sound even on the carpeted floor.

Oh. Crap. Mr. Cork.

He wore huge orthopedic shoes that made plenty of noise when he walked. He'd known I was going to be in the bathroom the day I was attacked, and I suddenly realized why the weird spicy smell I'd caught a whiff of down in the dark tunnel had seemed so familiar.

It had been Mr. Cork's cologne. The same cologne that swirled around me now, almost masking the underlying odor of rot.

The decay funk was so thoroughly clouded by his horrid perfume that you wouldn't realize it was there if you weren't looking for it. But now that I knew to look, it was amazing I hadn't caught it before. *Mr. Cork* was the source of the stink, not Clarice's horrible breath. Which meant he'd been there that day in the library, and down in the catacombs. I was betting it also meant he was the source of the evil vibe, not the hallway he urged me toward with his disturbingly bony hand.

"Principal Samedi! We're in here! Help!" I screamed, following my gut.

If I was wrong and Mr. Cork was telling the truth, I'd probably just doomed Gavin and myself to death or worse, but I couldn't seem to help myself. The feeling that Cork was the real baddie was so strong that the words leapt out of my mouth of their own accord.

Which turned out to be a good thing, though also pretty pointless. Principal Samedi didn't have time to reach the door before Mr. Cork showed his true colors big time.

"It's too late for help." He shoved me between the shoulders with surprising strength. It sent me crashing into Gavin, and the pair of us fell into the dusty brown hallway.

We landed in a tangle on the dirt floor and just barely had time to look over our shoulders before Cork slammed the door closed. The feral snarl on his face, paired with the satisfied gleam in his evil, sunken eyes, pretty much banished any lingering shred of doubt that *he* was one we needed to be afraid of.

Gavin lunged for the handle, but the entire door vanished into thin air. He fell back to the floor, grunting as he bit the dirt.

"Are you okay?" I reached over to him, but he was already on his feet.

"He's the one," he said, dusting off his robe with a slightly dazed expression. "How did you know?"

"His shoes and his smell. You know that rotted smell we noticed in the library?"

"Yeah."

"That's what he's hiding with that cologne, but I guess he has to reapply pretty often to keep it covered. Even with him standing so close, I didn't notice it until he opened the door and the draft blew the stench around." I turned to survey the hallway in both directions. The evil vibe wasn't as strong as it had been with Cork standing behind me, but it was still there. Wherever he'd sent us, I knew it wasn't somewhere we wanted to be. "He's *definitely* the harvester."

"No doubt. And he *definitely* isn't going to want us telling anyone about it." Gavin took a long look to our right and left. "We have to find a way out of here."

"You think he's going to come get us?"

I shivered, though it actually was pretty warm in the hallway. The flaming torches on the wall heated the air as well as provided light... not that it really mattered. We might as well have been fumbling around in the dark for all the good seeing did us right now. The hall truly seemed to stretch on forever in both directions. It was impossible to know which way to run, or if running would even do us any good.

Gavin sighed. "Either he's coming back for us to make sure we don't talk, or..."

"Or what?"

"Or he doesn't think we'll ever find our way out of here," Gavin said, the hint of defeat in his eyes.

"If there's a way in, there has to be a way out, right?" I asked, forcing the old PHS Peachpit spirit into my voice. Geez, I never realized there were so many real-world applications for cheerleading experience. I was beginning to think *Spirit Inspiration and Positive Thinking* should be a required course for all freshmen. "Besides, we have to be somewhere in the school. How far could this go if—"

"We might not be. If Mr. Cork is as powerful as I think he is, he could have sent us somewhere else. To a different place, a different time, maybe even a different planet."

"I think you've been watching too much Sci Fi channel," I said. "No one said anything about time travel or *Star Wars* stuff during *Magical Behaviors*."

Gavin actually grinned a little as he started down the hall to our right. I'd been feeling more of a left vibe, but at this point it seemed like a good idea just to get moving. "But wouldn't it be cool if there was life on other planets? Or if magic could help us travel through time?"

"No. Aliens are scary and time travel is always bad. Haven't you ever watched Saturday morning cartoons or those old movies with the short guy?"

"The short guy? That's descriptive."

I sighed. "You know, the short guy, the one who used to be on that TV show in the eighties? He had these hippie parents but was in love with Ronald Reagan?" Gavin's blank look told me he didn't spend his spare time watching Nick at Nite reruns. Probably too busy learning magic and swimming and doing his homework and responsible stuff like that. His loss, clearly. "Whatever. Point being, the space-time continuum always gets interrupted and the world gets destroyed or you create an alternate reality or marry your mother and cease to exist or something like that."

"That's gross."

"Totally. This is why we should stay in our own time and space and—"

"Wait a second." Gavin grabbed my arm. I froze beside him. "Do you hear that? What is that?"

I definitely heard something, but couldn't have begun to guess what was making the noise. It was like a giant broom swishing through a puddle of partially solidified Jell-O. Kind of a swish, splash, gurgle sound with a little jiggle at the end. "I don't know, but... it sounds like it's getting closer."

"Which I'm guessing isn't good." Gavin turned in a slow circle while I squinted my eyes, glaring into the space ahead of us, then spinning around to check behind. But nothing had changed. The hall was deserted, and the air as still and stale as it had been when we first fell inside.

I was getting ready to suggest we keep moving and hope for the best when something instinctual urged me to look up. After all, hadn't I just learned a lesson from Principal Samedi, the bat woman, about neglecting to check the vulnerable overhead area? And how many horror movies had Piper forced me to watch where something fell on the stupid half-dressed heroine and ate her alive because she was too busy freaking out and clutching her skimpy nightie to make sure the ceiling was free of gravity-defying vampires or psycho killers hiding in the attic or...

Giant, slime-covered maggot creatures. So *that's* what the white squirmy things on the door had been.

I didn't even waste time screaming before grabbing Gavin's arm and taking off at a sprint. Thankfully, he didn't waste time asking questions either. He just kicked it into high gear and raced down the hall beside me. You gotta love a guy who can lead, but who also isn't afraid to follow.

Good for him he was so liberated. Otherwise, the mondo maggot would totally have had him for a late-night snack.

FIFTEEN

In the event of a maggot infestation, douse the affected area with alcohol and seek immediate medical attention. Though maggots have been used in the treatment of human wounds for centuries, they can severely damage or destroy the Undead.

—*First Aid for the Undead*

Maggots seething, here they come
From the fly, we're all undone
It is the way of the maggot, the way of the maggot
The way of the maaaaaaggoooooot.

—*"The Way of the Maggot," Fleshrot, Alternative Zombie Volume 6, Hits of the 1990s*

———

"What the hell is that? A giant worm?" Gavin asked as the thing landed on the hall floor with a thunderous squish that made the ground shake.

"I'm thinking maggot," I panted, running even faster. From the slushy Jell-O sounds behind us, the maggot-worm was wasting no time starting its pursuit. "They eat dead things, right?"

"Do you really think of yourself as a dead thing?"

"Well, no," I said, struggling to talk and run at the same time. "But I probably would if I were a giant, hungry maggot. Besides, Principal Samedi warned me about maggots. They're our only—"

"Natural predator. Yeah, I know. But I read somewhere that doctors are using them to treat infected wounds in humans."

"Really?"

"Yeah, because they'll only eat dead flesh and leave the healthy stuff alone," Gavin gasped, risking a quick look over his shoulder before pushing himself into a full-out sprint. "It's because overuse of antibiotics has made people resistant...to...normal treatments...or something. But since our flesh is all dead and not...vulnerable to infection, I—"

"Are you seriously talking about this while we're running for our lives?" I was breathing so hard from trying to keep up with Gavin and his much longer legs that I wasn't sure he would understand me. But he did—and then he started laughing.

The boy was clearly insane, which made me like him even more. What that said about my own twisted psyche, I didn't want to know.

"I guess." He laughed again. "I've never really run for my life before. It's nothing like in the movies."

I could only grunt my agreement because, at that point, I was beyond banter. My lungs burned, and a weird metallic taste crept up the back of my throat, making it harder and harder to swallow. I can safely say I've never run so hard or so fast. I would have been hopeful that Gavin and

I could eventually outdistance the thing behind us if only there had been anywhere to run *to*.

But the hallway just stretched on and on, with no end in sight. There were no turns, no doorways, no nothing. The only point of entry or exit appeared to be the tunnels that popped up every so often overhead, like the one our maggot friend had oozed out of, and those weren't going to do us any good. We couldn't defy gravity and, even if we could, the chance we might run into one of white-and-gooey's friends while crawling around in said tunnels would have kept me right where I was.

Still, "where I was" wasn't much better, and it was getting worse with every second.

"We have to do something. There has to be a way out." I forced the words out despite the ache deep in my lungs.

"How? I don't see any doors, do you?"

"What about magic?" I asked. "What about your root?"

"Samedi took it when she brought us into her office," he said. "I could try to open a door without it, but—"

"Try! God, try!" I screamed, wondering why the heck he hadn't tried before. This was not the time for a crisis of faith in his abilities!

"I can't! I need time to chant one of the longer spells." Gavin sucked in a deep breath, but I could tell it wasn't as easy as it had been a few seconds ago. We were both running out of steam. "That thing would be all over us before I was halfway through."

Argh! No way. This couldn't be hopeless. I *refused* to

be ingested by a giant maggot. It was just too gross for words. What would they write for the obituary? *Perky ex-cheerleader with fabulous natural blond hair consumed by giant worm?*

"Ex-cheerleader," I muttered to myself, the bare hint of a plan forming in my mind. I was only an *ex*-cheerleader because DEAD didn't have a cheer squad, not because I'd lost any of my mad cheering skills. I was still Karen Vera, the most fearless flyer the PHS JV cheer team had ever known.

There had been girls on the squad who thought the only reason I topped the pyramid was because I was the smallest girl in the ninth grade. But I knew better. Now it was time to prove I was more than a runt with a decent toe touch.

"You ever seen a basket toss?" I glanced over my shoulder at our maggot friend. He was getting closer, but not too close. This just might work.

"That thing where they throw cheerleaders in the air?"

I nodded. "Usually it takes two people, but we're going to try it with one. When I give the signal, make a basket with your hands and get ready to throw me as hard as you can."

"Throw you where?"

"At that thing," I panted. "Over its head, not, like, in its mouth. I'm going to distract it while you get to spelling."

Saying the words out loud made the idea a heck of a lot more scary. What was I thinking? Sure, this would buy

Gavin time, but how was I going to get *off* the back of the maggot once I got *on*? Not to mention the fact that this stupid plan involved actually laying hands on a *maggot*. A giant, *slimy* maggot. I didn't even like to grab spoons out of the garbage disposal or fish hairballs from the shower drain, and I was thinking of riding something that fed on rotten flesh and garbage?

"That's crazy! I'm not throwing you at—"

"Do you have another plan?" I asked, praying he had something else, *anything* else.

But instead of spouting plan-like wisdom, he just sighed. "No."

"Then what other choice do we have? This will give you the chance to work the spell to summon a door."

"But, how are you—"

"I'll figure out a way to get back to you." I prayed the words were true. "Come on, we don't have much time. I can't run much longer."

And I couldn't. My muscles were already burning. If I pushed myself any harder, I wouldn't have the leg strength left to really launch myself into the air. And I needed to *launch*. No way did I want to fall a few feet short of my target and end up in Slimy's mouth. This critter had some serious pincher action going on that looked like it would hurt. Big time.

"Karen, I really don't—"

"Now!" I grabbed hold of Gavin's shoulder as we both ground to a stop. Thankfully, once again, he didn't hesitate to act and act fast. His hands dropped into a cradle just as I slid around in front of him and reached back to grab onto his elbows. Seconds later I'd bent my legs and jumped up, positioning my feet on Gavin's hands.

We were a loaded weapon, ready to fire.

"Now? Throw you now?" Gavin's voice held a trace of hysteria. *Finally*, he was losing his cool. And it only took staring into the face of a giant maggot quickly closing in on our position, wicked pinchers snapping in anticipation of a meal, to make it happen.

"Wait, not yet. Wait!" I had to yell to be heard over the moist sucking sounds of the creature wiggling down the hall, but I had a feeling I would have been screaming anyway. I wasn't just a trace hysterical, I was full-blown *freaked the heck out*, but it was too late to rethink this Karen-throwing plan now.

Our maggot friend was ten feet away…seven… five …four…

"Now! Throw me now!"

"Now?"

"Yes, now!" I shrieked, a sound that became a scream worthy of a horror movie as Gavin bent his knees deep and then shoved me into the air.

For a few seconds I was weightless and free, liberated from gravity in a way I'd only ever experienced at the very top of a kick-butt basket toss. Whether it was Gavin's manly muscles or just the abundance of adrenaline pumping through his system, I certainly couldn't fault the boy's throw.

I sailed up and over our maggot friend's head before it could flinch, easily avoiding both pinchers and creepy bulbous eyes, and landing with a squish on its surprisingly firm back.

For some reason, I'd expected its body to be soft and spongy, but it wasn't. It wasn't that slimy either, so who knew where the wet, sucking Jell-O sounds were coming from. Maybe the underbelly was squishier? Call me crazy, but I was hoping I wouldn't find out.

"Ahhhh!" I slammed my fists down on the creature's back a few times, screaming bloody murder, but it turns out I needn't have bothered. Mr. Not-So-Squishy was plenty disturbed by having me on his person—er, maggot.

He bucked and thrashed, halting all forward movement toward the yummy dead boy in front of him in an attempt to get the dead girl on top of him *off*. Turns out maggots *really* don't like having people on their backs.

They are much like unbroken horses or rodeo bulls or my father in that way. Dad never gave me a piggy-back ride around the house. *Never*. Even when I was a little kid. He refused to play any breed of fun, roughhousing games until the boys were born, which is clearly sexist and has probably caused me some emotional scarring. No doubt I'll end up talking about that with my therapist some-day…after we work through all the post-traumatic stress caused by my dying on the sidelines of a football game, getting sent to a zombie school where one of my teachers turned out to be a killer, and wrestling a giant maggot.

"Karen! I think I've almost got it!" Gavin was busy down the hallway a few dozen feet away and had already summoned a blue light from the wall—amazing how times flies when you're beating on the white, spongy flesh of something that wants to eat you.

"Okay!" I screamed back, hoping some sort of brilliant getting-down idea was going to fly into my head the same way the leaping-on-the-maggot's-back idea had.

But it was hard to think clearly, what with all the thrashing and high-pitched screeching (my screeching, not the maggot's). I was fairly certain it couldn't make sounds, or it would have made some already. Maybe it didn't have vocal cords? Did baby worms really need vocal cords? Or were maggots baby flies?

Now that I thought about it, I was pretty sure they *were* baby flies. Hadn't Principal Samedi said something about watching out for flies who liked to lay their eggs in Undead skin because that's how maggot infestations got started?

The thought made me cross my fingers that we didn't run into this baby's daddy. I'd looked at a fly under a microscope in sixth grade science and could totally do without seeing *that* up close and personal again. I was also pretty sure fly puke was made of acid, and having your flesh slowly scalded away by fly puke would probably be an even worse way to die than being eaten alive by a—

"Karen!"

Oh crap! Why couldn't I stay focused? What was it

about high-stress situations that made my mind go into tangent mode? You'd think it would be the opposite. You'd think being terrified or seconds away from certain death would help me to *focus*, for god's sakes.

Focus...I had to distract the maggot's *focus*. But how?

I didn't have a weapon, or a flashlight to shine in its eyes, or even anything to throw that might distract it long enough for me to slide to the ground and make a run for it. I didn't have anything in the pockets of my robe except for a tube of lip-gloss and the remnants of the brain bar I hadn't finished earlier in the library and—

The brain bar! It wasn't dead flesh, but it *was* food, and this thing was definitely hungry.

Clinging to one of Not-So-Slimy's fat rolls, I dug into my pocket and yanked out the bar, struggling not to fall off as he continued to buck and thrash. But once I'd freed the slightly sticky remains from the wrapper, I had a major moment of doubt. A brain bar wasn't very big, half a brain bar was even smaller, and this baby's mouth was *really* big. What if my little smackerel didn't even register on its digestive radar?

"Karen! Hurry, I can't hold the door for long!" Gavin was clinging to the handle of a plain-looking brown door that kept fading in and out like a bad television signal.

I had to get down there ASAP or we'd both be out of luck, because it didn't seem like Gavin was going to leave without me. (I know! Isn't he the most amazing guy in the history of the entire world? I mean, the heroes in books and movies never leave the heroine behind to be eaten by a giant maggot, but I was betting in real life a lot of guys would have hauled butt first and waited for the damsel in distress never.)

The thing beneath me gave a mighty squirm and smashed its head into the ceiling, sending dust raining down on both of us. It wasn't getting any happier about having a passenger and I was out of time. It was the brain bar or bust.

Refusing to think negative failure-type thoughts, I scrambled up closer to Mr. Maggot's eyes and peered down, waiting until it reared up again before hurling the brain bar between its pinchers and into its damp and gooey mouth. For a second, nothing happened. I had pretty much decided I was maggot food when the creature suddenly snapped its mouth shut and froze in mid thrash.

I didn't wait to see how long this incapacitation-due-to-yummy-brain-bar was going to last. I just jumped up and ran, straight off the edge of its face. My legs and arms churned as I fell, as if they could somehow carry me further away from the monster behind me by swiping at the air. Time slowed to a horrible crawl, only jolting back to full speed when I landed with a groan—not three feet from the giant pinchers, close enough to feel the heat generated by maggot mastication. I winced as I stood. Pain shot through my left leg, but I didn't dare take even a second to assess whether my ankle was really broken or just felt that way.

"Open the door!" I screamed as I half limped, half ran

to where Gavin was still struggling with the door. Behind me, baby maggot screeched (I guess it could make sounds after all; there went the no-vocal-cord theory). "Hurry!"

"I'm hurrying!" he shouted back, tugging on the handle until sweat ran down his forehead and into his eyes. "It's stuck!"

Smushy Jell-O noises signaled that our friend was once again on the move. We had to get the door open! Now!

I lunged for Gavin's arms, putting my hands over his and tugging with all the strength left in my body. Finally, after seconds that stretched into horror-filled oh-my-god-we're-about-to-get-eaten hours, the handle gave under our combined efforts and the door swung open toward us. We dove for it.

Gavin and I fell to the floor inside the cool room just as a very hacked-off worm slithered straight into the still-open door, shattering the aging wood and snapping the door right off its hinges as it barrelled on down the hall. The door disappeared into thin air before I could even guess where we'd ended up, but that didn't stop me from sending up a mental shout of triumph. Wherever we were, it had to be better than wherever we'd been a few seconds ago.

"We're okay. We're okay," Gavin was chanting under his breath. And turns out, we were.

The floor beneath us was the cool, smooth tile found in the first-floor DEAD classrooms, and the air smelled comfortingly of zombie-kid campus: a mix of fried brains from the cafeteria, industrial lemon cleaner, and chlorine from the school pool. It was fairly dark in the room, but then again, it *was* the middle of the night. It would have been weirder if the classroom lights had been on, right?

So... we were safe. We'd escaped death by maggot and would live to tattle on Mr. Cork and hopefully recover the missing brains of Trish and his other victims before it was too late. This was the moment to take a deep breath and heave a sigh of relief... so why was I suddenly wishing for a one-way ticket back to endless-tunnelville?

"Cork!" Gavin mouthed the word as he grabbed my hand and tugged me under a nearby lab station. We were in one of the chemistry labs, which meant there was room under the large table for both of us to hide. Thank. God.

Because Gavin was right. I smelled the funk of Cork seconds before heavy footsteps sounded in the doorway to the classroom. Had he found us? Or was it just dumb luck that we'd ended up within striking distance of the most evil, skanky skeleton on campus?

"Death in the temple would have been easier and far less painful. I can assure you both of that." More heavy footsteps, but Gavin and I didn't move a muscle. There was always the chance he was talking to someone else, and besides, we had nowhere to run—Cork was blocking the only way out. "I was attempting to do you a favor, Mr. McDougal, but you always have been far too clever for your own good."

Okay, so there went the *maybe he wasn't talking to us* theory. Argh!

We scrambled out from under the table and faced our dastardly English teacher across the rows of tables. At least there were a few obstacles between us and him. Maybe we could find another way out, or Gavin could open another door, or someone would interrupt Cork before he could deliver on the threat of a harder, more painful death.

"Or maybe you'll finally die and quit making things more difficult," Cork said. "I cast my vote for the last option, Miss Vera, especially considering Mr. McDougal is far too weak to open another door under nothing but his own personal power. I'm actually shocked he managed to open one at all."

I wasn't. Gavin was the bestest, and Mr. Cork was clearly just jealous.

"The bestest?" Cork laughed, a mean, narrow sound that made my fingernails itch. "Really, Miss Vera. I expected better vocabulary from someone worthy of an A- in my class."

Unholy crap on a moist cracker. He was reading my mind—because I was sure I hadn't said the word "bestest" aloud.

"And no, Mr. McDougal, Miss Vera can't tell how scared you are. You're completely pulling off the part of the heroic little man."

"How the heck is he—"

"It's the brains," Gavin said, grabbing my hand and pulling me a little closer. "He's been eating the brains, at least parts of them. It's given him the power to read our thoughts."

"Clever, young Gavin." Cork clapped his skeletal hands. "Isn't he clever, Miss Vera?"

"Um, yes." Was that a rhetorical question? Did I even need to answer out loud, since he was mind-reader man?

Ugh, I didn't like that idea. At. All. It was sort of like Mr. Cork was going through my underwear drawer, but a thousand times worse. After all, my panties were all very nice and worthy of being found dead in. My thoughts, however, were not.

"It's part of what makes him so attractive, that cleverness," Cork said, giving Gavin a slow, up-and-down look that would have been way more appropriate for ... um ... *me* to be giving him. "Wouldn't you say so, Miss Vera? That young Gavin's confidence and intelligence are as much a lure as his undeniable good looks?"

This time I didn't care if it was a rhetorical question—Cork was getting a non-rhetorical answer. "Actually, I think you're a complete perv. Gavin is still underage, not to mention a dude."

"A dude?" Cork smiled, a baring of his teeth that somehow made him smell even worse.

"Yes, a dude," I said, backing away as Cork shuffled closer to where Gavin and I stood. "I'd like to be cool with it since I believe in people's right to love freely and all that, but I'm just not okay with it in this situation. Maybe because you're old and evil as well as a dude."

Cork laughed, a moist, wheezing sound that reminded me of the maggot's slither. "Old and evil, perhaps. But I'm no 'dude.' I'm as much a female as you are, Miss Vera."

And then he started taking his skin off. Yes. His skin. Off.

SIXTEEN

In his poem "The Darkest Hours," Akori explores
the transitory nature of time and its effect upon the
Undead world versus the human world. The con-
trast of the silence of the "nonbeating heart" with
the pounding "hooves of the Roman horses" serves
to emphasize the stillness of eternity versus the fre-
netic pace of human life.

—Excerpt, Karen Vera's A- poetry assignment,
Mr. Cork's 1st period freshman English class

The rotted, spongy skin oozed off Mr. Cork's bones with
the ease of a slicked-up sunbather coasting down a water-
slide. Really, it was more amazing that the stuff had stayed
on than that it was coming off. It was *that* gelatinous and
just plain gross.

"Stay back, it could be poisonous," Gavin shouted,
tugging me away from the green fluid rushing out from
around Cork's feet in the wake of the skin sloughing. We
scuttled all the way to the wall behind us, only stopping
to stare at the freak show when there was nowhere else to
run.

"You should see your faces. Priceless." Mr. Cork giggled as he stepped out of the puddle of his skin and clothes,

proving he really was way more disturbed than the average dude.

Or *chick*, as he'd have us believe. He'd said something about being female, but who could tell when he/she wasn't much more than a pulsing mass of sickly-looking organs in a shell of thin, fragile bone?

"Indeed. I've been forced to make do with grotesque, mostly male disguises. No one has been able to see me as a woman for many, many years. Far longer than either of you have been alive." She was sad now, her hideous brown eyes bulging in the raw, red tissue of her face, proving she was moody enough to be female.

Not to be a jerk, but we females *are*, as a sex, more moody. That's not sexism, that's truthism. Boys don't run crying from rooms one-fifth the amount girls do. It's our hormones, I think. They're clearly more unstable than boy hormones, which is totally not fair and one of the many things I'll be taking up with god if there is one and I get to a place where I'm allowed to talk to him/her/it.

"But all of that is about to change." Cork sniffed, and a sliver of grayish-green dripping from her nose crept back up into her skull. It was all I could do not to start dry heaving when I realized it was a little globlet of her brain trying to escape, not something more mundane and mucusy. "The spell I work tonight will finally allow me to regain my strength *and* my female form."

"You can't work that spell. Those girls don't deserve to die," Gavin said.

"No, they didn't deserve to live on after death."

Mr. Cork—um, *Mrs.* Cork—sounded very at peace with her decision. She obviously had no issues with killing Trish and the other girls and intended to carry on with her very bad self. Argh! We had to do something, had to find some way to call for help. Maybe if we just screamed bloody murder for long enough, someone would hear. We were quite a distance from Samedi's office, but there had to be guards wandering the halls.

Reading my thoughts, Cork turned and swiped a hand toward the open door behind her, sealing us inside the lab. She whispered a few words under her breath before turning back to Gavin and me. "There now, we won't be disturbed."

"Listen, there has to be another way to work this out," Gavin said, foolishly trying to reason with the insane person in front of us. Didn't he realize you can't reason with crazy people? That's why they called them *crazy.* "Trish and Kendra and Penelope are good people. They've never—"

"They are bodies, nothing more, and should have been returned to the earth as soon as the black magic animating them was terminated." Cork waved a dismissive hand in the air, scattering little spots of blood across the table in front of her. "My sister is the one who committed an unforgivable offense against those poor girls. It's an abomination, really, the way she plays with innocent lives."

"You mean Principal Samedi?" Gavin asked, catching on way faster than I would have. Suffice it to say there was *no* family resemblance between this thing and our principal, but the connection was confirmed when Cork nodded sadly and sniffed another piece of her brain back into her head.

Ew. Gag. Blechk. I couldn't think about that anymore or I really would yack.

"Theresa has turned her back on everything our coven used to stand for. She shouldn't be allowed to practice magic, just like those girls should never have lived on after—"

"Who are you to decide who should or shouldn't be alive? Or Undead, or whatever?" I asked, finally getting that this was a Deprogrammed thing. Cork was cool with killing Trish because she wasn't naturally Death Challenged, and that just sucked. It was nothing more than a convenient excuse to kill.

"You misunderstand, Miss Vera. *I* decided nothing. The Great Mother is the one who decides. Or should be allowed to decide. Theresa must be taught a lesson." Cork moved closer, and I could feel Gavin's urge to run in the way he gripped my fingers so tightly our bones rubbed together.

Under other circumstances, the feel of his hand in mine would have been enough to make me have a crush-induced spaz attack of major proportions, but I was beyond the point of boy-girl feelings. And that made me sad ... and angry. Who was Cork to wreak havoc on the school and kill people and traumatize me and everyone else?

"I am one of the first, child. One of the very first." Closer and closer she shuffled, the hand she trailed across the lab tables leaving a trail of crimson on white. "I walked the earth long, long before your parents' parents were born, and I will remain when you are truly dead and gone."

"Karen isn't Deprogrammed, Cork—"

"Please, call me Amisi."

Gavin pushed on, ignoring the walking skeleton's attempt at an introduction. "If you kill Karen, you're violating everything you just said you believed in. If the Great Mother made Karen Death Challenged, who are you to take that right away?"

"It is not a right," she spat, anger flashing in the mad depths of her eyes. "It is a privilege, one that Karen has scarcely earned. And of course you, little sir, are as much an abomination as the rest." Her hand rose and her bony fingers curled. "Now come here to me, children. Let us end this before you are forced to suffer any further."

"I'm not suffering. I'm cool." My eyes searched the area around us, looking for some sort of weapon. I did my best not to think about what I was doing so that Cork wouldn't catch on.

"There is no weapon that can wound me," she said, still moving inexorably closer, like a run in your tights you just know won't be stopped by massive amounts of clear nail polish. "At least none that you could wield."

Argh! The mind reading thing was really annoying.

"It will be over soon enough, when you no longer possess a mind to—" Her words ended in a howl as Gavin grabbed a beaker from the shelf behind him and hurled it into her face.

It was just a normal glass beaker, not filled with acid or anything cool like that. But apparently the shards-of-glass-stuck-in-tender-flesh factor was still plenty painful, because Cork screeched like a banshee. Gavin and I darted around her and hustled toward the door. Thankfully, my ankle was feeling much better than it had post–maggot jump so I had no trouble hauling tail. I reached the door at the same time as Gavin. We both pounced on the handle, tugging and pulling, but it wouldn't open.

"She must have put a spell on it or something." I spun around to see one very hacked-off skeleton lady lurching toward us. "Hurry! We have to—"

"I can't get it open. She's right, I don't have that kind of power. I'm all tapped out from making the other door appear." He tugged at the handle a few more times, then turned around with a wild look. "The brains! They've got to be somewhere in here. We have to find them."

"They are? We do?" Okay, I was lost, but Gavin seemed like he had an idea, which was better than anything I had, which was…nothing, other than a vague plan to scream and maybe jab Ms. Cork or whatever her name was in the eyeballs a few times while she ripped my brain from my skull.

I figured mauling her as I died was the very least I could do.

"Why else would she be here?" Gavin asked, darting across the room toward the giant walk-in refrigerator near the teacher's desk. I tailed him, shrieking as Cork flung some sort of blue light at our heads. We ducked just in time to save our skulls, but the projector screen behind us wasn't so lucky. The entire thing caught fire and burned to white ash within the space of a few seconds.

"Oh crap, oh crap," I whispered under my breath, even as my mind began making mad bargains with god.

If he/she/it would just let us live, I promised not to give him/her/it a hard time about girl hormones or anything else when I got to the afterlife. By the time we reached the fridge, I'd thrown in a few other promises involving a free pass on the world hunger issue and a bunch of other stuff that I normally wouldn't have budged on.

But I just *really* didn't want to check out. Not here, not now, not when we had survived so much.

"Hurry, get inside." Gavin wrenched open the door to the walk-in fridge and shoved me in just as another burst of blue light exploded right next to us.

"But we'll suffocate, or get hypothermia or—"

"Or live for a few more minutes. She won't be able to cast magic through stainless steel," he said, slamming the door closed and flipping the lock, shutting us in the walk-in fridge with all the baby pig corpses and bovine lung tissue like so much dead meat. "Besides, we're dead. We don't have to worry about hypothermia."

"Oh yeah," I said, teeth chattering regardless.

Maybe it was a mental thing, or just a side effect of all the unadulterated fear. There was certainly plenty of that to go around. Ms. Cork was pounding on the door like the mad hatter she was, leaving dents the size of baseballs in the metal. She was amazingly strong for a skeleton. It would only be a matter of time before she smashed her way in.

"Come on, help me look for the brains." Gavin rummaged through the drawers on the far side of the fridge. I turned to help him, squealing as Cork smashed another fist into the door.

"She looks so weak. I mean, she can barely walk—how is she—"

"It's the brains. They have to be close by." Gavin stopped trying to be neat and started tearing drawers from the wall. "If she's eaten part of them, she'll have established a connection. She'll be able to draw strength from them when she needs it, like batteries. But if we can find them and—"

Another mighty crash rocked the room, and even the frozen air around us seemed to rattle.

"Oh god." I scrambled back from the cabinet I'd just opened. "I think I've found them."

Gavin rushed to my side, only to sigh and turn away again. "Those are pig brains."

"Look again." I grabbed Gavin's sleeve and pulled him back to the cabinet. "Look at the reflection in the mirror behind the jars. It doesn't match."

He froze, blue eyes squinting into the "reflective" back of the cabinet.

"*And*, do you see *us* in that mirror anywhere?"

"You're right. It's not a mirror. I didn't even notice." Amid much smashing and crashing from outside, Gavin pulled down the jars of pig brains concealing the jars of girl brains behind the glass. "Sorry."

"Don't worry about it." Secretly, however, I really liked the fact that Gavin had no problem admitting when he was wrong. A lot of boys are weird about that, like the fact that they have boy parts makes them incapable of making a mistake or something.

"We've got to find something to break through the glass."

"It doesn't slide open?" I asked, running my fingers along the outer edge of the cabinet. "There isn't a latch or—"

"We don't have time to find out." Mrs. Cork punctuated Gavin's words with a particularly brutal one-two punch. "Here, this should do it." Gavin grabbed a frozen pork loin from one of the back shelves (looked like Miss Newhouse, the chemistry professor, kept her snacks as well as her class supplies in her fridge) and brandished it like a baseball bat. "Stand back."

"Be careful, don't shatter the jars the brains are in or it might—"

"I won't," he said. "Move back."

"For real, Gavin. If they're damaged, we don't know if—"

"Karen, please!" He turned to glare at me over his shoulder and in that split second I could see our entire future stretching out ahead of us. Hundreds of years of blissful yet argument-filled coupledom in which he would probably yell my name in that exact tone of voice no less than a gazillion times.

It would have made me smile, if Ms. Cork's fingers hadn't broken through the door at that very second.

"Hurry!" I screamed, grabbing another pork loin from the shelf and running to the door, where I proceeded to whack Cork's bony hand as she did her best to grab hold of the latch. Hopefully her blue magic didn't work when she was being beaten with frozen meat, or Gavin and I were both toast.

"I'm hurrying," Gavin yelled. "Watch yourself, don't let her touch you."

"Right!" As if that needed to be said. No way was I letting Cork any closer, not as long as my muscles were functioning.

The sound of glass breaking behind me made me jump, but I didn't stop pummeling for a second, not even when I realized I had no idea what Gavin planned to do with the girls' brains. I mean, we had to get them back to their owners, of course, but he'd acted like finding them would save our skins as well as the harvested victims'.

"I've got them!" Gavin's words were followed by a little squishing sound and then a wail from outside the door.

"No! You worthless little bastard!" Cork pulled her

hand back with a scream of pure agony. Whatever Gavin had done, it certainly seemed to have worked.

I spun around, ready to congratulate him, but all my happy shiny words shriveled and died in my mouth. Turns out I was not capable of speech while watching the boy I was almost certain I was in love with chew a huge mouthful of brains.

People brains. Because Trish and Penelope and Kendra were people. People Gavin knew and allegedly liked. Even Trish had been growing on him, I could tell.

But, like them or not, he was still eating them. *Eating* them.

In that moment, I was more grateful than I would have thought possible that I'd never kissed those slimy, gray-matter-smeared lips or the criminal attached to them.

"Karen, wait," he said, though it sounded more like "Krr, wrrt" since his mouth was so obscenely full.

But I didn't wait. I ran. Out of the refrigerator, past the spasming body of Cork on the floor outside, and out the now-able-to-be-opened classroom door, determined not to stop until I was as far from all of this madness as a girl could get.

SEVENTEEN

Put your right hand inside the circle you have created using a piece of yarn or string and chant the words of the illusion spell three times. Then, wrap the yarn or string around your wrist or ankle and secure with a firm knot.

The string should be left in place until such time as the caster wishes the illusion spell to fade. Should the string fall off or be lost or destroyed, the caster will have between two and four hours to recast, or the illusion will be lost and the caster's true identity revealed to the human world.

—*Basic Illusion Spells and Traveling Protections*

After a brief seminar refreshing the student body on the proper casting and maintenance of illusion spells, each student will be granted a three-day pass to visit friends and family. Classes will resume on Monday.

—*Friday morning announcement, DEAD High*

———————

Friday afternoon, six days later…

"I don't see how you could have ever left them in the first place. They're adorable!" Trish was so grossly in love with my little sister and brothers that I was actually starting to get jealous. We'd been down in the trips' basement play-room for hours.

I mean, I love the trips and all, but they aren't *that* great. No one who spits up on other people as often as Kimmy, Keith, and Kyle do deserves to be more adored than yours truly. Especially since *I* was the one responsible for saving Trish's life.

If I hadn't found Principal Samedi and tipped her off to where to locate her psycho skeleton sister and the hot junior boy chowing down on illegal brain food, who knows if there would have been enough of Trish's brain left to successfully reanimate her body?

Hmm... maybe *that's* why she was so gaga over the trips. Maybe Gavin or Ms. Cork had consumed the part of her brain that was necessary for understanding that small, wriggly people who smell funny are really not all that cool.

"But I'm so glad you're coming back to school," Trish added, smiling at me for a second before turning her atten-tion back to Keith. "It's just not the same without you." Keith was playing some baby game that involved slam-ming his head into Trish's knee and giggling like a maniac. Trish was giggling too, but even Kimmy was shooting them "give me a break" looks from where she was making a pretend pickle sandwich over at the Little Tykes kitchen. Maybe it was a boy and brain-damaged person thing.

"It's only been a week," I said, though I was secretly pleased to hear how desperately I'd been missed.

"It seems like forever. I was so pysched when I heard we were all getting a three-day pass this morning. We should have gotten one on Monday. School was pointless this week. The entire ground floor was blocked off because of the investigation, and the Science and English classes had to be held in the library."

"All at the same time?"

"Yes! It was so crowded it was impossible to concentrate, even though the guy who replaced Mr. Cork, Mr. Eden, is pretty cute for an old guy." Trish heaved a put-upon sigh. "After a couple days, the teachers all gave up trying to educate us and made us read the school handbook instead. It was so boring I almost wished my brain was still missing."

"Ugh, not funny," I said, but we both laughed a little.

"No. But I did wish you were there. It would have made the torture much more bearable."

"Even though you've got a ton of new BFFs?" I asked.

From what I'd heard, Trish, Kendra, and Penelope were the new celebrities at school. Turns out having your brain snatched and then being reanimated several days later is a recipe for instant popularity. Trish's sketchy past had been all but forgotten—as it *should* have been a long time ago.

We'd chatted on the phone earlier in the week and Trish had told me all about what went down with her first roommate. The poor girl had gone on an ice cream bender, thinking the worst she'd have to deal with was a little gastric discomfort. Unfortunately, however, she'd been one of the one-in-one-hundred Undead with a severe milk allergy. She'd gone into toxic shock and never recovered. Principal Samedi had known Trish wasn't to blame and the investigation had been a formality, nothing more. But in the true tradition of teenagers everywhere, the gossips had gotten hold of the story and twisted it until Trish was a murderer.

It stunk that she'd nearly had to be murdered herself to remove the stain on her rep, but no one ever said high school was a nice place. What was nice, however, was that Trish had finally started to change her view on the entire DC vs. DP controversy.

Yes, she still thought it sucked that the groups were treated differently, but she was starting to see that a lot of her rage against the machine might have just been rage against being unfairly judged. Between her juvie past and the unfortunate business with her first roommate, she'd had a hard time fitting in, and that was bound to color one's point of view.

Now she was getting a fresh start, and I was too.

Principal Samedi had told everyone about the hex spell and allegedly most people felt pretty bad about the way they'd treated me. I still wasn't expecting to be Miss Popularity when I returned to school—since my part in solving the mystery of the missing brains was being kept strictly under wraps so as not to encourage any other students to get their Scooby Doo on—but I'd probably have a few options when it came to finding a seat in the cafeteria. I mean, at the very least I could ride the wave of Trish's newfound stardom.

"Darling," Trish drawled, rolling her eyes, "they are *not* BFFs. There is only one BFF."

I grinned, satisfied by the reminder that I was still the most specialest. "You're just kissing up because you want me to let you smuggle a television into our room."

Trish was moving in with me as soon as I went back to DEAD on Monday. Clarice had been suspended for thirty days for working minor black magic against another student and would be in a room all by her lonesome when she returned.

She wouldn't have been returning at all, however, if she and Darby hadn't convinced Principal Samedi they were trying to save Trish by using her necklace to track down the person who had stolen her brain, not looking for ingredients to use in their own forbidden magic. The fact that the spell they'd worked had led them through the snake door and into the catacombs where Cork—aka Amisi Samedi—had been lurking, spying on her sister's new coven, worked in their favor.

But I still wasn't buying. Clarice was evil. Not even her sob story about it being a cheerleader driving a pink convertible who had caused the wreck that killed her parents could soften my heart. I still thought she should be strung up by her toes in the lunchroom and pelted with goat eyeballs. It was the least of the punishments I could imagine for making the entire school hate me—except for Trish and Gavin, of course. (Trish because she was in the room when Clarice was casting and was therefore immune to the hex, and Gavin because of his gris-gris bag.)

Ugh. Gavin. I couldn't even think about him without getting all sick to my stomach and kind of dizzy with despair.

"Karen, are you listening? We *need* TV. I really don't think it's fair to—"

"We can watch it in the common room like everyone else," I said, pulling my thoughts away from the gorgeous yet gross Gavin and tugging Keith away from Trish's knee before he gave himself brain damage. One zombie per family was plenty, thank you very much. He whined for a few minutes, but I distracted him with his blocks. "At this point, I'm not risking any illegal contraband. We need to be perfect little angels for the rest of the semester."

"Yeah, you're probably right." Trish grabbed Kyle as he ran by and pulled him into her lap. She really had a baby problem. I was going to have to get her out of the playroom soon or she might decide to leave school and volunteer to become Mom's nanny or something. "And no TV means I'll get to play more classic rock, the better to complete your musical education."

"Yippee. Grandma music."

"It's not—"

"Yeah, yeah, whatever." I jumped to my feet and crossed to the foot of the stairs. "Mom! Trish and I are getting ready to come up."

"Okay, be right down," Mom yelled back.

"We are?" Trish's disappointment was clear on her face.

"I'm starving, aren't you?" I asked, hoping the lure of leftover brain-and-kidney pie would trump the lure of babies.

"Actually, I ate right before I left school. They passed out snack-packs after the illusion spell assembly so—"

"And we've got the new episode of that vampire show TiVo-ed. I heard the girl ditches the wolf guy and goes back to the Undead arms of her first true lurve."

"Oh my god, finally!" Trish squealed loud enough to earn a glare from Kimmy. "Undeader is so better. What was she thinking, hooking up with a guy who turns into a dog?"

As if a guy who sucks blood was a big catch? Call me crazy, but I'd take a zombie over a wolfman or a vampire any day. We might eat animal brains and have cold skin, but overall we acted like the humans we were before death. We didn't get all frisky when we smelled blood or want to chew on your shoes or anything like that.

"Okay, buddy, give me kisses." Trish stole a few spitty baby kisses from Kyle before setting him down on the floor next to Keith and racing me up the stairs. "Come on, Karen. Get your hustle on."

So, bloodsucking hotties trump both food and babies. Good to know. I'd have to remember that in the future. Trish and her mom were already making plans to come to our house for Thanksgiving, and I certainly didn't want to lose Trish to the basement of eternal babble and drool for an entire day.

"Your food's ready. Just grab the bowls out of the microwave," Mom said as we emerged into the kitchen, wiping her hands on a towel before heading down the stairs to take over trip-wrangling duty. "Oh, and that boy called again."

"What boy?" Trish asked.

"No one important." Good going, Mom. I would have given her the patented why-must-you-speak-in-front-of-my-friends glare but she was already halfway down the stairs.

"It's Gavin, isn't it?" Trish squealed and did a little dance over to the microwave. "He's *so* in love with you."

"He is not." I grabbed two Seltzer waters—one of the few drinks kosher for the Undead—from the fridge.

"Oh he is too. He's asked about you like every single day, *and* been calling, I see." She shot a glare over her shoulder. "I can't believe you didn't tell me."

I shrugged. "It's no big deal."

"It is so a big deal. He's the hottest guy in school, and he's in lurrrvve with you."

"He is *not*." I fetched the TV trays and prayed Trish would give it a rest already.

"Hate to repeat myself, but he is too."

"Whatever. Even if he were, I'm just not into him."

Trish let the spoons she was holding clatter into our

bowls before fixing me with a look that left no doubt she questioned my sanity. "You have to be joking."

"No, I'm not. I just don't see the appeal." Yeah, right. I'd more than seen the appeal, I'd been totally head-over-heels and imagining the way he'd yell my name when we were old married people.

But that was *before* I'd seen him with a mouthful of illegal brains.

Principal Samedi had let him off the hook for nibbling on forbidden cranium fruit. I was guessing they had worked out a deal where he didn't tattle on her for trying to work an illegal suspended-animation spell and she didn't deliver him to the High Council for munching the brains of other zombies. But I couldn't forgive him. All that time, I'd thought he wanted to help Cork's victims, but he'd really just wanted to snack on Trish and Kendra and Penelope himself. It was so disappointing it made my teeth ache. I'd been *so* convinced he was one of the good guys.

"Wow … you really are the vainest person I've ever met." Trish set our bowls on the trays and then grabbed hers and headed into the den. "That's going to cause you grief in later life."

"What?" I asked, trailing after her.

"I mean, no offense, Karen, but you're not going to find anyone hotter or smarter or nicer than Gavin. If he's not good enough for you, then—"

"That's not it at all." I sighed. "Can we just change the subject?"

Keeping the secret of Gavin's brain-eating was driving me crazy, but I didn't want to tell Trish. Principal Samedi had asked me to keep mum about it, and also not to say anything about Mr. Cork really being her evil sister. I didn't see that I had any choice but to do what Samedi said. I mean, I still had to go back to school and, after my encounter with her sister, I was sure Samedi would know if I'd broken my promise. Gavin had said the mind-reading thing was only possible because Amisi had eaten zombie brains, but I wasn't going to risk it. If there was even a chance all ancient zombies could read minds, it was enough to keep my mouth firmly closed.

Besides, I didn't want to freak Trish out. If I knew that someone—even a totally hot and crush-worthy someone—had eaten part of *my* brain, I would have had a debilitating skeeve attack. Trish didn't need any more stress in her life after everything she'd been through.

"Fine." Trish set her tray down and flopped back onto the couch. "But when you're old and alone and your looks start to go and everyone talks about what a stuck-up chick you always were in school, don't come crying to me."

Okay, maybe she did deserve more stress.

I was getting ready to hint that she shouldn't speak of things she didn't understand or risk committing Stupidity in the First Degree when the doorbell rang.

"Crap! I've got to go get Mom." I assumed my illusion spell was working (although I still looked the same to myself, other Undead, and my immediate family), but

I didn't want to risk opening the door. It wouldn't do for the neighbors to see the girl whose memorial service they'd attended almost two weeks ago signing for packages.

"Wait up," Trish said, rushing to the curtains. "It might be my mom. She said she'd stop by on her way home from work and drop off a few things for tonight. She hinted she'd been baking."

"Sleepover goodies?"

"Yeah, she's pretty amazing with brains, for a woman who... Oh. My. God."

"What? What is it?" I asked, immediately anxious. What if one of my friends from my old life had decided to stop by to visit my mom? Would I be able to pull off the "new nanny hired to help with the trips" cover we'd decided on?

"No, the question is *who* is it." Trish turned from the curtains with a wicked gleam in her eyes. "I think you better come take a look. Your loverboy is here."

EIGHTEEN

Love stanks,
When it's your skin you're rotting in,
Love stanks,
When the reaper's not your friend.
Zombie love ain't love at all
Cause lovin' you just stanks.

—*"Love Stanks," by Empty Cranium, Undead Power Ballads of the 1980s*

———————

"What?" Fear clutched at my throat. Surely she couldn't mean—

"Come on, Karen, let me in," came a muffled voice from outside the front door. "We need to talk."

Holy. Crispy. Squid brains. It was Gavin. On my porch. Undead and in person.

My hand flew to smooth my hair before I could remind my addled hormones that this was *not* the boy for us. There were more important things in the world than good looks or a great personality or being brave enough to risk your life by waiting to go through a magic door until the girl you're with has leapt down off the back of a giant maggot.

Gavin had betrayed his own kind and deliberately misled me. I couldn't forgive that, no matter how many great things he had going for him.

"Crap, what should I do?" I shifted nervously from foot to foot. Should I go get my mom? Hide in the bathroom until Gavin got the hint and vacated? Get Trish to tell him it was never going to happen, à la third grade, when I'd sent my friend Betsy over to tell Craig Summer, the nose picker, that I didn't want to be his girlfriend?

"Let him in, you goob," Trish said, grabbing her food and heading back into the kitchen.

"No!" I snatched at her arm, intending to hold her prisoner. She couldn't just leave me here! Alone! With Gavin on the porch!

"Yes." She rolled her eyes and dodged my grab. "Don't be weird. I'll just go hang in the other room until you've talked this out."

"Don't go, I—"

"I'm going, Karen. Just chill out and talk to the boy. But know I *will* be trying to eavesdrop, so don't talk too loud." She disappeared into the kitchen.

Great. At least she was honest, but this put me in a very bad position. How could I tell Gavin I didn't want anything to do with him because he was a lousy, no-good brain eater when one of the girls whose brain he might have eaten was listening in the other room?

"I'm not leaving until you open the door, Karen," Gavin yelled, loud enough to attract attention if anyone was walking by.

Argh! I was going to have to let him in. I couldn't just leave him out there screaming a dead girl's name. But I wouldn't let him say a word about what had gone down last week. I'd tell him I had company and I wasn't interested in hearing anything he had to say. End of story.

I ran to the door, doing my best to ignore the full body flutter inspired by the thought of seeing Gavin face to face. He was a greedy brain muncher. I must remember that he was a gross, repulsive—

"Listen, I..." I froze in the doorway, completely stupefied.

Ohmygod, he was *so* not gross. He was still totally the cutest guy in the entire world and there was no way I was going to be able to resist drowning in the cerulean blue ocean of his eyes. He was a bug light and I a mosquito helplessly drawn to his killer glow. He was a cobra and I a mouse lured by his hypnotic serpent's dance. He was a—

"Um... can I come in?" he asked, in this soft voice that made my bones melt. What was wrong with me? There had to be something malfunctioning somewhere. Other girls were not this vulnerable to the lure of cute boy-ness. I probably had a hormonal imbalance or something. I'd have to get myself checked out by Dr. Connor as soon as I got back to school.

Assuming Dr. Connor was still around. She'd seemed pretty bummed out to learn her other great-great-granddaughter had been the brain harvester. She might have decided to take a vacation or something.

I wished *I* was on vacation. Then I wouldn't have to be *here*, staring at *him*.

"Sure. Yeah." I stood to the side and shooed Gavin in. "Wouldn't want the neighbors to see me," I added, trying to make it clear that this was the only reason I was letting him in.

"But you worked an illusion spell before leaving school, right? So you should be fine."

"Yeah, but...you can't be too careful." I tilted my nose into the air. He would not shake my resolve with logic or words or logical words.

"Oh. Right."

"Right." I slammed the door and turned to give him my best you-are-a-lower-life-form-unworthy-even-of-my-scorn glare. "What do you want?"

"Okay, guess we're getting right to it, huh?" Gavin sighed and leaned awkwardly against the doorway between the foyer and the living room, hands shoved in his pockets.

He was wearing dark blue jeans and a tight black sweater, making it even more difficult for me to resist drooling in appreciation. I'd never seen him in weekend wear. I mean, the boy made the DEAD uniform look good, but in normal street clothes he was...practically irresistible. And if I was honest with myself, it wasn't even the way he looked that floored me. It was just...him. His energy, his aura, the look in his eyes when he was looking at me—all that stuff.

Be strong! Think about his lies, and his nasty eating habits, and the way his lips were all shiny after he munched Trish's brains.

Ugh. Way to go, inner voice. Draw attention to his lips why don't you?

"Do you know what I mean?" he asked. "Can't you just think about that?"

Think about what? Crap! He'd said something and I'd missed it because I was too busy thinking about his stupid lips. Bad call on that one. I'd be better off thinking about poor little puppies who'd been run over crossing the street. Or maybe kittens. I didn't really care for dogs. They were so slobbery and smelly and they chewed on everything and I already had the trips to do all that, so—

"Karen?"

"What?" I snapped the word with more frustration than intended, angry at my stupid brain tangents more than at Gavin, but he didn't know that.

His eyes flashed and he threw up his hands. "Fine, I guess I should just go."

"Yeah, maybe you should." I struggled to ignore the horrible sinking feeling in my gut. I really didn't want him to go, but it was for the best. Our love could never be. We were like Romeo and Juliet if Romeo had been a cannibal and Juliet hadn't died after taking that poison ... or plunging a knife through her heart or however she offed herself in the end. I'd tried to block that whole last part out. It was just too depressing and tragic.

Kind of like what was happening right now.

"Fine." Gavin headed back to the door.

"Fine," I said, barely resisting the urge to clutch at his

sweater and tell him to stay and fight with me some more. Even fighting with Gavin was more fun than having fun with a normal boy.

"I'll just show myself out."

"Good, you should."

No, you shouldn't! I love you! (But I didn't say that out loud.)

"I was stupid to think you'd even try to understand," he continued as he reached for the door. "You're obviously too selfish."

"Selfish?" What? Was he on crack? I rushed to the door, grateful for an excuse to shove it closed. "I'm not the one who pretended to be a good guy when all I really wanted was to snack on innocent girls' brains."

Oops. I'd spilled the beans. Hopefully Trish wasn't listening too closely.

"I never *planned* to do that," he said, the outrage in his voice pretty darn convincing. "It was the only way I knew how to stop Amisi."

Oh. "It was?"

"Yeah, she was drawing strength from the brains, but I thought if someone else consumed part of her power source…" He shrugged, obviously ashamed of what he'd done, whether he'd had a choice or not. "I figured it would slow her down, and it did."

"Oh." Wow… now I felt like such a jerk. A selfish, only-thinking-about-my-own-grossed-outedness jerk. So I guess Samedi had let him off the hook because he was only trying to help, not because they'd worked out some sort of non-tattling arrangement. "I didn't know that it worked like that."

"I didn't know for sure, either. I thought it would weaken her enough for us to escape. I had no idea it would kill her. I don't know if I would have been able to—"

"She's dead?" I was more relieved than I probably should have been. I mean, bad guy or no bad guy, I didn't want anyone dead. Maximum security prison for life would be good.

"Yeah. She'd been mostly dead for a while, anyway. She'd worked too much black magic, and it made her flesh deteriorate faster than normal." He shoved his hands back in his pockets, making his manly swimmer muscles bunch beneath his sweater. "Principal Samedi said she would have been too rotten to survive if she hadn't shoplifted Mr. Cork's skin and started harvesting brains when she did."

"So there is a real Mr. Cork?"

"Um ... not anymore."

"Oh." Poor Mr. Cork. "God. What a witch."

"No kidding." He shifted uncomfortably as the conversation suffered from Awkward Pausitis.

"So ... yeah." I strained to think of what to say next, how to apologize for shunning him when all he'd done was take one for the team to save my life. I felt like such an idiot, and I didn't see how Gavin could forgive me. I'd judged him without knowing all the facts, just like the entire school had judged Trish. I'd thought I was better than that ... guess not.

"Amisi's name means 'flower,'" he said with a little snort. "How wrong is that?"

"Very wrong." I laughed, but it was a tight, strangled sound.

Another long pause ensued. Geez! Why couldn't I just say I was sorry? He'd been calling for the past week, so he obviously wanted things to be cool between us. But how cool? Just friends cool, or something more cool?

"Yeah ... so everything's good then?" Gavin asked. "You don't think I'm a repulsive freak?"

"No way," I hastened to assure him. "And I'm sorry I jumped to conclusions."

"And then wouldn't take my phone calls," he added.

"That too." I was pretty sure I blushed bright red, but Gavin didn't notice because he was already turning toward the door. He was leaving!

"Okay, see you Monday."

"Okay ... Monday," I said, watching him leave with my nonbeating heart squirming around somewhere in my small intestines.

I couldn't let him go! Not like this! But what could I say? I couldn't very well confess my eternal devotion in the foyer, not when it seemed like he only wanted to be friends. Argh! This was so hard! If only we'd been allowed to kiss—or not kiss—that day in the library, at least then I'd know for sure if Gavin had any more-than-friendly feelings for me at all.

"Bye." He waved, smiled, and then the door closed and ... it was over. The last chapter had been written. The book had been closed, taken back to the library, and was well on its way to being checked out by someone else.

"She who hesitates is lost," I muttered to myself. It was one of my dad's favorites quotes. He'd been using that one on me since I wasn't much older than the trips, but only now did the full weight of its wisdom settle upon my thin shoulders. I'd hesitated. And now, I was lost. Sniff.

I was turning back to the living room, mourning the fact that chocolate therapy was now forbidden to me, when a pillow hit me in the face.

"What are you thinking? Go after him," Trish hissed.

"I can't," I said, though I knew she was totally right.

"You must!"

"I can't. I can't go out in the front yard. Someone might see."

"You're under an illusion spell, no one is going to—"

"I don't trust the illusion spell!" I screeched. I knew I was being totally unreasonable, but I *didn't* trust the illusion spell just yet, and even more importantly, I was scared to death. What would I say to Gavin if I did go after him? I hadn't had a clue two minutes ago, and I didn't have any more of a clue now.

"Then go wait at the back door, I'll go get Gavin and tell him to meet you there," Trish said, shoving me toward the back door as she ran toward the front. She'd reached the door and was about to pull it open when Gavin shoved inside, grabbed Trish, and came terrifyingly close to kissing her.

Terrifying for me, at least. I swear, I almost puked my heart up from where it was lurking in my small intestines.

"Oh, man. Sorry," Gavin said, his hands flying away from Trish's face and his lips kind of sliding off her ear as they stumbled and nearly fell down.

"It's cool." Trish grinned as she finally regained her balance. "I think you were looking for her."

And then she pointed to me, and Gavin turned in slow motion, just like in the movies—I think his hair was even ruffled by an invisible wind and maybe some sort of rock ballad started to play. And then he was crossing the room, and then he was cupping *my* face in his abnormally large but unbearably attractive hands, and then ... he was kissing me.

And it was even better than I had imagined. Even with my best friend looking on, giggling like a madwoman. It was a first kiss to die for. Luckily, I was already dead. So I didn't die.

I just sighed and kissed him some more.

About the Author

Stacey Jay is a workaholic with three pen names, four kids, and a decidedly sick sense of humor. She loves creepies, crawlies, blood, guts, gore, and of course, romance. In her spare time she enjoys wild things like running with scissors and driving her minivan five miles over the speed limit. Learn more at http://staceyjay.com.